Cirsova

P. ALEXANDER, Ed.
Mark Thompson, Copy Ed.
Xavier L., Copy Ed.

A Fantasy Novelette of the Macabre

Short Stories of Thrilling Suspense

POETRY

Winter Issue
2018

Vol.1, No 10
$10.00 per copy

Cover art for Jeopardy Off Jupiter IV by Anton Oxenuk, Copyright 2018. The content of this magazine is copyrighted 2018 by Cirsova and the respective authors. Contents may not be reprinted physically or electronically except for purposes of review without prior permission. Cirsova and Cirsova Heroic Fantasy and Science Fiction Magazine are trademarks of Cirsova Publishing. Please support independent science fiction: buy copies for your friends, family and Dr's offices!

LOST TRAILS 2

Forgotten Tales of the Weird West

Edited by
Cynthia Ward

AVAILABLE FROM AMAZON, BN.COM,
AND OTHER FINE RETAILERS

Jeopardy Off Jupiter IV

By SPENCER E. HART

The Jovian Patrol Boat Nevada has received a distress call from a small vessel near the moon Callisto! Was the explosion on the Masuyo that left the ship on a fatal trajectory an accident, or are more sinister forces at work targeting the VIP on board?!

Osiris Jackson turned from daydreaming about his upcoming shore-leave on Callisto. There was a sharp pinging in his ear. He quickly turned dials to get from the commercial frequencies to the radio bands reserved for official use by the Guard and the governments of the Four Moons.

"Vessel *Masuyo* calling any Jovian Guard vessel near Callisto. Repeat, vessel *Masuyo* calling Jovian Guard."

Jackson flipped a toggle switch and spoke into his microphone. "This is Jovian Guard Patrol Boat *Nevada*, Lieutenant Jackson speaking. We receive you *Masuyo*, over."

"This is Captain Morita. May I please speak directly with your captain?"

Osiris frowned slightly as he replied, "Please stand by, *Masuyo*."

Well, Jackson, you were just thinking how dull this cruise out from Ganymede has been, he thought.

Osiris got up from his seat and walked to the hatch of the small radio compartment. The magnetic soles of his shoes clicked on the decking as he went out into the corridor.

"Commander!" he hollered in the direction of the control room. "Message from vessel *Masuyo* coming in on official frequen-cy. Captain Morita wants to speak with you directly."

Seconds later, Caraffa, a mustachioed man in the gray duty uniform of the Jovian Guard, came out into the central corridor. He leaned back in the direction of the control room and said, "All right, Whittaker. Just keep us on course for now."

As he approached, the commander said, "What's this about, Jackson?"

"I don't know sir. The captain of the *Masuyo* wanted to speak to you."

Caraffa's olive-hued face tightened in concentration for a moment. "There are no Guard ships named *Masuyo*. Let's find out why a civilian is on an official channel."

Osiris followed the Europan officer into the radio room and indicated the waiting microphone.

"This is Commander Caraffa in command of the Jovian Guard Patrol Boat *Nevada*. Am I speaking with the captain of the *Masuyo*?"

"Yes, Commander. This is Captain Morita of the vessel *Masuyo*. We request assistance. There has been an... incident... aboard our ship."

"What sort of incident, Captain Morita?" Caraffa asked.

"Our rockets failed to fire as we were about to enter orbit around Callisto for our return home. The *Masuyo* will miss the world entirely and continue on its current heading."

Commander Caraffa gripped the microphone tighter. "Can your engineer alter your course at all?"

Captain Morita's voice hardened. "Sadly, our drive-man Sato must be dead. The engine room reads as vacuum."

"Please relay your position and velocity, Captain."

Morita gave a series of navigation figures.

Caraffa jotted them down on a pad near the radio. "Captain, I will do what I can. But why did you not give a general distress call to all ships in the vicinity?"

"Our passenger requires a certain amount of... discretion... regarding the current situation," said Morita. "It would be best not to say more over the radio, even on this frequency."

"Acknowledged, *Masuyo*. Please wait for further communications from us in a few minutes."

Commander Caraffa gestured to Osiris. "Jackson, raise Callisto Base and advise them of the situation. We might have to delay our refueling stop. See if they can get us some help headed in the direction of the *Masuyo*."

"Yes, sir," saluted Osiris as he again took his seat in front of the console.

The commander stepped out into the corridor and called, "Whittaker! I need you to run some course calculations based on our remaining fuel supply."

About five minutes later, Caraffa returned to the radio room.

"Raise Captain Morita again, Jackson," he ordered.

Osiris tuned to the previously used channel. "Vessel *Masuyo*, this is Patrol Boat *Nevada* calling, over."

Without delay, Morita's voice responded. "This is *Masuyo*. Please go ahead."

Caraffa took the microphone from Osiris's hand. "Captain Morita, this is Commander Caraffa. We calculate we have enough fuel left to intercept your course in 2.75 standard hours. We will render what aid we can once we arrive, over."

"Message received, Commander. We look forward to your arrival," said Morita.

Caraffa toggled the microphone off and turned to Osiris. "So what did Callisto Base have to say about all this?"

Two-and-a-half hours later, Osiris sat in the control room as the *Nevada* neared the *Masuyo* and decelerated to match velocity.

He stared through the forward telescope at the growing egg-shaped orb of the Callistan ship. It was a small passenger-type, perhaps half the size of the *Nevada*, lacking the larger engines and fuel tanks of the Guard vessel.

"Lieutenant Whittaker, how long till we catch up to them?" asked Caraffa, sitting at the engine controls.

The pale flight engineer from Io looked up from his gauges and dials.

"At our current rate of deceleration, nine minutes and twenty seconds, Commander."

"Lieutenant Jackson, get back to the radio room and raise the *Masuyo* again. Let them know to expect us in a few minutes."

"Yes, sir," answered Osiris.

As he began to turn away from the telescope, Osiris caught something out of the corner of his eye.

A second, much smaller spot, had appeared near the *Masuyo*. And the spot was moving, the distance increasing.

"Sir!" he called, "Looks like there's an object near the *Masuyo*, drifting away perpendicular to her course."

The commander turned his head towards Osiris. "Any idea what it is, Jackson?"

"No, sir," answered Osiris, "but it's pretty small compared to the ship."

"Get to the radio and get the *Masuyo* on. Let them know what you saw. Maybe they have some idea what it could be."

"Yes, sir!"

Jackson backed away from the telescope and left the control room through the hatch.

Once back in the radio room, Osiris called the other ship.

"*Masuyo*, this is the *Nevada*. We are approaching your position and will be alongside within a few minutes. However, we have spotted a small object near your ship. It seems to be moving away from you, over."

The voice of Captain Morita came over the radio, "It must be Nishio, our co-pilot. He does not answer my radio."

"A man is outside the ship?" asked Osiris.

"He had gone to try to reach the engine room from the outside and inspect the damage. But Nishio has not spoken for a few minutes now."

"*Masuyo*, please stand by while I alert Commander Caraffa."

Osiris stood up and made his way back to the control room.

"Sir!" he called once he got to the hatch.

Caraffa didn't look up from his delicate piloting, now that the ships were so close together, but said "Yes, Jackson?"

"Contacted *Masuyo* as ordered, sir. Captain Morita says that's a man out there."

"Whittaker! Can we adjust course slightly and intercept that man, then still reach the *Masuyo*?" asked Caraffa.

"Give me a minute, sir," Whittaker said as he did some quick calculations.

"Make it snappy, Lieutenant. Closing in fast."

The engineer looked up. "Righto. We can do it by a quarter-second burst from the port nose thruster."

"Jackson! Get out to the airlock and suit up. You'll have to be the one to get that man and bring him in."

"Yes, sir!" Osiris said as he turned back down the corridor. He felt the *Nevada* shift course as Caraffa fired the thruster.

Jackson went past the radio room and stopped at the row of space suits fastened to the bulkhead opposite the airlock hatch. He took down the one with the big numeral "3" on the chest, and put himself into the suit, legs first, then arms, and zipped up the front.

Osiris donned the bulbous helmet, screwed it into the neck-ring resting on his shoulders, and reached up to turn on the radio mounted to the helmet.

"Jackson here, sir," he called into the local circuit. "All suited up and about to enter the airlock, over."

Caraffa's voice came back via the tinny speaker inside the helmet, "Roger, Jackson. We have just about caught up with the man. Proceed into the airlock."

Osiris turned the big wheel on the inner hatch and pulled it open. Once inside the tiny compartment, he closed the inner hatch then pushed a bright red lever upwards to where it said "VENT PRESSURE" on a plate affixed to the bulkhead.

The air was sucked back into hidden tanks, and Jackson spun the wheel on the outer hatch. Pushing it open, he carefully turned to face the inner hatch, grabbed a couple of metal rungs just outside, and pulled himself into space.

He was still facing the *Nevada* and put his magnetic boots on the outer hull. Reaching to one side, Osiris pulled the end of a steel tether from a spool fastened to the ship and clipped the line to his space suit.

Turning his whole body to face away from the ship, Osiris tapped his radio again. "Jackson here. I'm outside and secured to a tether. All ready to go."

"Wait until I give the word," responded Caraffa. "Then you jump straight out and use your thruster-gun to get to that man. Grab hold of him, then tug on your line twice to trigger the winch to bring you both back to the airlock."

"Roger, Commander. Waiting for your word."

Osiris got his legs positioned beneath him and looked out into space.

Facing away from Jupiter and now tens-of-thousands of miles away from its fourth major moon, Callisto, only specks of light from a couple of the minor moons and some stars were visible in the blackness.

"Get ready, Jackson. Three... two... one... JUMP!"

Osiris kicked off with all his might, enough to snap the magnetic soles loose from the hull. The tether fed out behind him.

At first, he didn't spot his target, but he soon saw the silvered form approaching from ahead and to his own left. The relative motions of the *Nevada* and the man were close but not exact, so Osiris drew the thruster-gun from his left leg and gave it a few spurts.

Just do like back in rescue training, he thought.

Closing in, Osiris could see his target was tumbling slightly, arms and legs spread wide.

Osiris grabbed hold of the Callistan, used the thruster-gun to stop the tumbling, and twisted the man around to look at him.

The other man's radio was smashed where it was fastened to the helmet. And one of the air lines from the back tank was raggedly torn loose.

Osiris looked into the man's face through the frosted helmet.

The visage of Nishio was twisted, mouth open, eyes wide.

The man was dead.

Osiris looked away and gave two quick tugs on the line.

en minutes later, the *Nevada* had matched velocity and was stationed a hundred yards off the *Masuyo*'s port side, so that the airlocks faced each other.

Commander Caraffa stood over Osiris's shoulder as the lieutenant sat in front of the radio console.

"Yes, Captain Morita," Caraffa said into the microphone. "Your man Nishio is dead. Perhaps caught himself on some damaged area, smashed his radio and tore his air hose."

"I see. It is a tragic loss; he was a fine young man," came Morita's voice through the speaker.

"Captain, I would like to send my two men over to your ship to assess the situation. I must remain with the *Nevada* to make sure we do not drift apart."

"Agreed, Commander. I look forward to meeting them."

Caraffa put down the microphone, and Osiris toggled it off.

"Jackson, I want you back in your space suit," said the commander. "I'll send Whittaker over with you. Rig a couple of the suit-tethers from our airlock to theirs."

"Yes, sir," said Osiris as he stood up.

A few minutes later, Whittaker and Jackson had crossed over to the *Masuyo* and clipped their tether-lines above the Callistan ship's outer hatch.

"Okay, Jackson. I'll go in first. Let me do the talking as I'm the senior man," said Whittaker. "The Callistans are sticklers for protocol."

"There were a couple in my class at the Guard Academy. I understand," Osiris answered.

Osiris waited outside while Whittaker cycled through the airlock.

At last the light over the hatch changed, and he turned the wheel and entered. While the compartment pressurized, he prepared himself to face the Callistans.

The inner hatch swung open, and Osiris saw Whittaker standing, helmet tucked under one arm but still in his suit.

Nearby stood a Callistan man in a fancy uniform. The man was shorter than Osiris, but broader. He had the black hair and light complexion Osiris thought typical of the few Callistans he had encountered before. The man's face showed the lines and strains of responsibility, but it was hard to guess at his age.

Osiris removed his helmet and stood at attention behind Whittaker.

"Welcome aboard the *Masuyo*, gentlemen," began the Callistan. "I am Captain Morita."

Whittaker saluted. Osiris did the same.

"Thank you, Captain. I am Lieutenant Whittaker of the Patrol Boat *Nevada*. This is Junior Lieutenant Jackson," said Whittaker, making a small gesture.

"Lieutenant," Morita said, "before we begin our work, there is something you must know."

Osiris stood as stock-still as Whittaker.

"The passenger aboard the *Masuyo* is a very important and honorable personage. Knowledge of her travels is somewhat... confidential, and might impact relations among the Four Moons. That is why I radioed the Jovian Guard directly to request assistance.

"If you will remove your space suits and follow me, please, gentlemen," Morita continued, "I must notify the Lady that help has arrived."

After removing their space suits and hanging them on the bulkhead near the hatch, Osiris and Whittaker followed the captain down the central corridor. They turned a few feet into a short cross-corridor and stopped in front of a closed door.

"Our passenger compartment. Lady Takagi and her attendant are within," said Morita.

Captain Morita tapped lightly on the compartment door.

"Kimura-san?" he said.

The door slid open to reveal a woman.

Her hair was as black as every Callistan Osiris had ever seen, but it was piled and twisted up onto the top of her head in an artful way. Her skin was much lighter than his own, lighter than Commander Caraffa's, almost as pale as Whittaker, but with a hint of gold to it. She wore a modest green dress with the skirt down to her heels and a wide yellow belt around her narrow waist.

The woman answered, "Yes, Captain?"

"Kimura-san, these are the men from the Jovian Guard who have come to our assistance. Lieutenant Whittaker and Junior Lieutenant Jackson. Gentlemen, this is Miss Kimura, attendant to the Lady Takagi."

Her head moved almost imperceptibly in first Whittaker's direction, then Jackson's.

Osiris's breath caught in his throat as her eyes met his own. They were as dark as the deepest reaches of space and glinted like distant stars.

Her mouth opened a tiny bit, then she tilted her head downwards and broke the connection.

"Pleased to meet you, gentlemen," she said softly as she made a slight bow from the waist.

Captain Morita nodded, and Whittaker and Jackson followed suit.

"Kimura-san," Morita said, "please inform Takagi-sama that help has arrived. We will give further information once we have evaluated the situation more."

"Hai, Captain. I shall inform the Lady at once."

She slid the compartment door shut, but Osiris thought he caught a twitch of her head in his direction during the last instant before it closed with a sharp click.

"So, gentlemen," began Morita as he led them towards the control room of the *Masuyo*, "let us get to work."

"So, chaps," Whittaker said, "the *Nevada* doesn't have much fuel left, but we do have enough to at least brake the *Masuyo* and keep it from continuing farther out from Callisto's orbit."

Commander Caraffa's voice sounded from the radio speaker in the *Masuyo*'s control room, "We'd just have to keep the situation stable until more help arrived, then."

Osiris stood nearby in the control room of the Callistan ship, listening as Whittaker, Caraffa, and Captain Morita discussed what options they had.

"Sirs?" Osiris asked, "Are we sure there is no way to get the *Masuyo*'s rockets going again?"

Morita let out a breath. "Nishio was unable to enter the drive room from the outside, and since it is a vacuum in there we cannot get to it from inside either."

"So the braking plan seems our only option at this point," came Caraffa's voice. "Whittaker, come back to the *Nevada* and prepare the tethers; Jackson, I want you to stay on the *Masuyo* and keep on top of things there."

"Yes, sir," said Osiris.

Half-an-hour later Jackson was in the control room of the *Masuyo* with Captain Morita. Whittaker had unfastened the suit-tethers and returned to the *Nevada*.

The Guard vessel had pivoted 180 degrees in relation to the Callistan ship and now faced back towards Jupiter.

"Magna-grapples read as secure, Captain," Commander Caraffa's voice came across the radio.

Several minutes had passed since a pair of thick steel cables had been gently extended from the *Nevada* towards the *Masuyo*. Powerful electromagnets on the ends of the lines had latched onto the passenger ship's hull.

"Good, Commander. How long until you attempt the rocket-firing?" asked Morita.

"As soon as you aboard the *Masuyo* are all secure for acceleration, Captain."

"Please wait. I must inform the passengers to be ready."

Morita stood up and turned to Osiris. "Lieutenant, please remain here until I return."

"Yes, Captain."

Osiris strapped himself into the co-pilot's station as Morita left the compartment.

A vision of the dead face of Nishio flashed into his mind.

Shouldn't worry, Osiris thought. *Soon as we brake the ships, we just wait for help. Callisto Base will come through.*

Osiris stared out the front viewport into the darkness.

With a violent lurch, he felt his body pressed into the seat.

We're moving! But too soon!

A loud bang sounded from the central corridor, followed by a sharp cry.

Morita wasn't strapped down!

The acceleration increased, and Osiris felt like he was being squashed.

There was a deep vibration through the hull.

Then Osiris felt his body being thrown to the side of the chair as the force cut off.

Clearing his eyes, Jackson looked up at the viewport again.

The stars were slowly spinning round and round.

He unfastened his belts and stood up. His magnetic shoes clicked, and he made his way towards the hatch into the corridor.

Captain Morita was crouched in the passageway, cradling his left arm.

As Osiris approached, Morita rose to his feet.

"Lieutenant, what is the situation?" he said.

"The ship is tumbling slightly, sir. Somehow the braking maneuver must have gone off too soon."

Osiris glanced at the captain's left forearm. It looked bent at an odd angle.

"Sir, how badly are you injured?" he asked.

Morita's face became expressionless. "That does not matter now. We must see to the passengers at once."

Osiris hesitated. "Shouldn't we radio the *Nevada?*"

"After we have been assured that the Lady is safe and well, Lieutenant," Morita said, "we will do that. Please follow me."

Osiris trailed in his wake down the corridor.

The captain knocked on the door with his good arm.

"Kimura-san?" he called. "Is all well inside? The Lady is unhurt?"

"One moment," a voice said from inside the compartment.

The door slid open, and she stood there. Her head swiveled slightly towards Morita's injured arm, then towards Osiris.

He almost caught a glimpse of her eyes as she lowered her gaze.

Osiris suppressed his disappointment. *I wish she'd look up*, he thought.

"Takagi-sama is well. We were strapped down and safe, Captain."

"Praise the heavens," Morita said.

"Captain, are you hurt?" she again tilted her head slightly towards his arm.

"It is nothing worth mentioning."

"Takagi-sama will be pleased to hear it," she said.

"Please excuse me, Kimura-san. The lieutenant and I must return to the control room and contact the *Nevada*. Something must have gone wrong with the braking attempt."

"Be well, Captain."

The door slid shut.

Minutes later, back in the control room, Osiris was on the radio with the *Nevada*.

"We don't know why," relayed Whittaker, "but the rockets fired early and at higher thrust than planned. It took a bit to cut them off, but the grapples broke loose from the sudden strain. We're back to square one."

"Can the *Nevada* come back and rendezvous with the *Masuyo* again?" asked Morita. The captain's left arm was held straight at his side due to the splint he had allowed Osiris to affix once back in the control room.

Commander Caraffa's voice came from the speaker, "We don't have enough fuel. When the grapples broke, the courses of both ships diverged. The *Masuyo* was slowed somewhat, but is still moving away from the Four Moons. Meanwhile, the *Nevada* is drifting very slowly back towards Callisto's orbit."

"Has there been any word from other Jovian Guard vessels?" asked Morita.

"Not yet. We have radioed Callisto Base and requested any and all ships able to reach either of our vessels to come as quickly as possible."

"Sirs?" Osiris spoke up.

"Yes, Jackson?" said Caraffa.

"The *Masuyo* still has fuel in her tanks. If I could reach the engine room and see if the rockets can still be fired..."

"Nishio tried that, Lieutenant," said Morita, "and he was unsuccessful. In fact, it cost him his life."

"With all due respect, Captain, it is the safety of your passengers I'm concerned with," said Osiris. "We don't know when help is coming. I'm willing to risk it for their sakes."

"Your attitude is commendable, Lieutenant Jackson," Morita said. "What say you, Commander? He is your man. I will accept your decision."

"Jackson, I've never lost a man under my command," said Caraffa.

"Sir," Osiris said.

"I order you to be careful out there."

"Yes, sir!"

Osiris firmly planted his feet on the outer hull as he moved out of the airlock.

No suit-tether rig here, he noticed. *Must've never planned for regular EVAs.*

He drew his thruster-pistol and gripped it tightly.

Careful to make sure each step ended with the reassuring feel of a boot gripping the hull plates, Osiris made his way towards the rear of the *Masuyo*.

Coming around the last curve of the hull, Jackson spotted the hatch. It was open; Nishio must have gotten that far.

Osiris cautiously approached the opening.

No signs of external damage. No holes in the hull.

Gripping a protruding rung, Osiris looked into the airlock. The chamber was empty, and the inner hatch was also open.

Osiris stepped into the airlock and peered into the engine room beyond.

Wonder if the drive-man's body is still in here? What was his name again?

A hint of a shadow behind him made Osiris start to turn.

He caught a glimpse of a space-suited figure as something crashed into his helmet.

Osiris's ears rang as his vision blurred.

Blinking to clear his eyes, Osiris saw the space-suited man let go of a large wrench and lunge at him.

Getting a glimpse of the attacker's twisted face, Jackson remembered. *Sato—the missing drive-man! He must have killed Nishio!*

There was no time for further reaction as Sato grabbed onto Osiris's suit with one hand while the other reached for the back of his space helmet and his air line.

Osiris twisted and thrust an elbow back, jarring the grasping hand. Trying to dislodge the grip of his would-be killer, Osiris threw himself back towards the open outer hatch. Sato held on like a maniac, still grabbing for the air hose.

Osiris glanced down for an instant and saw the thruster-gun in his own left hand. Jackson pointed the gun and squeezed the trigger.

The jet of compressed gas hurled the both of them out the hatch and free of the *Masuyo* entirely. Their arms and legs all jumbled together, the pair tumbled out into space.

Osiris let up on the trigger, swung his left arm and gave it another blast while trying to twist around to face Sato.

The combined forces tore Sato's grip loose, and they drifted apart.

Osiris stopped his spinning motion with spurts from his thruster-gun and swiveled to face his enemy.

Sato had pulled out his own thruster and stabilized himself. With a last burst he charged back at Jackson.

Not this time, you rat! thought Osiris.

Jackson twisted the thruster-gun behind him then held down the trigger. The counter-charge sent him slamming into Sato chest-first.

Osiris released the trigger and lunged out with his right hand, striking Sato on the helmet. The drive-man clutched at Jackson's air-line, seemingly unfazed by the blow. Sato squeezed on the hose. Osiris strained and reached for the back of Sato's helmet.

Jackson felt himself beginning to go a bit woozy from the reduced air. His hand found the enemy's air hose running between helmet and backpack, and he yanked with all his might. Sato's hose gave way with a great rip.

The man flailed about as Osiris pushed him away, then released his grip.

The jet of escaping air sent the body back into a spin, drifting away from the ship.

As Osiris watched the form of Sato hurtling away into space, he noticed an odd patch of pure blackness off to his right. No stars shone there, or any other points of light, although a speck that might have been one of the minor Outer Moons was visible just beyond its edge.

Then the speck vanished, as if the black patch was growing larger.

"What is it?" whispered Osiris to himself. The answer came as he spotted a tiny flare of light shooting from a point near the center of the blackness.

A ship! A ship painted pure black as camouflage. Not growing larger, but getting nearer to the Masuyo!

Osiris tapped the side of his helmet and spoke, "Captain Morita? This is Lieutenant Jackson, sir."

The only answer was dead silence, not even the crackle of static.

Suit radio must have been broken in the fight with Sato, thought Osiris. *I've got to get back inside and warn them!*

Osiris turned and fired his thruster to get back to the ship.

Precious seconds passed. His magnetic boots clicked against the hull. He walked across the hull, back towards the main hatch as fast as he could manage. As he was about to re-enter the ship, Osiris turned and glanced to the side. The black ship was still getting closer.

A minute later, after letting air back into the closed hatch compartment and rapidly twisting the handle of the inner door, Osiris lurched into the central corridor of the *Masuyo*.

Osiris unfastened his helmet and headed forwards up the passageway.

"Captain Morita!" he called as he reached the control room.

The older man stood up from his seat, cradling his splinted arm and turned as Osiris stepped into the compartment.

"Lieutenant Jackson, were you able to reach the engine room?"

"No, sir. I was attacked on the way. By your drive-man, Sato."

Morita's mouth gaped open for a moment

before he regained his composure. "What? Then Sato has been alive all this time?"

"Not anymore, sir. He tried to kill me, and we fought. His body is floating away outside. But that can wait. There's a ship approaching. A ship painted all black."

Morita's face went hard. "Only criminals would have such a ship. Or... enemies. And the *Masuyo* is drifting without engine power."

The captain stared directly into Osiris's face. "Under no circumstances must the Lady be taken from this ship. Do you understand, Jackson?"

Osiris straightened to full attention. "Sir, it is my duty as a man of the Jovian Guard to defend your passengers even if it costs me my life."

Morita twisted his head towards the command station. "In that small locker behind my chair are two atom-pistols. Please retrieve them, take one for yourself and give me the other."

Osiris went to the locker and took out the guns. He handed one to Morita, who took it with his good arm.

"We must inform the Lady of the situation. Follow me to the passenger compartment, Lieutenant."

A minute later Morita gestured for Osiris to rap on the door. After a moment, the door slid open, and Miss Kimura stood there. Her face was inclined towards the floor.

"Yes, Captain?" she asked.

"Kimura-san, there is a problem. A ship of criminals is approaching the *Masuyo*. We will do our best to hold them off, but if we fail... Do you understand, Kimura-san?"

Osiris heard her take a deep breath.

"Hai, Captain. I will inform Takagi-sama at once."

As she slid the door shut, Osiris thought he saw her head turn slightly towards him. Just like before.

"Lieutenant, you must guard this spot between the passenger compartment and the hatch," Morita ordered. "No one must pass."

"Yes, sir," answered Osiris.

"I will take position in the corridor near the control room. That way, both of us can aim at the hatch and make a cross-fire."

The captain walked back up the passageway, and Osiris took a position where he had some slight cover by standing near the bulkhead across from the passenger compartment.

Long minutes passed.

He heard a click behind him and glanced back towards the passenger compartment.

"We are prepared, Lieutenant," said a familiar soft voice behind him.

Miss Kimura stood in the opened doorway. She quickly lowered her face again as soon as he turned his head.

Why won't she look me in the eyes again? he thought.

"Miss Kimura," he began, "why all the mystery? Who is the Lady Takagi?"

"Takagi-sama's husband leads the Takagi zaibatsu," she said. "Perhaps you have heard of it."

One of the largest industrial conglomerates on Callisto. Osiris wanted to smack himself for not making the connection earlier.

"Yes, I've heard of it. But why the secrecy? Surely more help would have come if the Captain had sent a general distress call?"

Miss Kimura's whole body stiffened.

"Takagi-sama is also cousin... to the Emperor."

Osiris's jaw dropped and he gaped dumbstruck for a moment.

"The Lady will not be taken by criminals," she said sternly, "nor will I."

Osiris noticed that a knife had appeared in her hand.

"What..." he mumbled as he stared at her still-downcast face.

A single tear floated free of her cheek as the door slid shut.

"They won't get past me," he said loudly to the closed compartment. "Do you hear? I'll stop them."

I hope. His mind whirled.

Minutes later, the waiting was getting on Osiris's nerves. *Why don't they just get it over with, already?* he thought.

He adjusted his sweaty grip on the atom-pistol, still trained on the hatch.

"Ahoy, vessel *Masuyo!*" blared the speakers from the control room.

This is it, Osiris thought.

"This is the Cutter *Bordeaux* of the Jovian Guard. Your mysterious friend turned and ran at the sight of us. Stand by for our arrival."

Osiris released a breath he had not realized he had been holding.

Osiris escorted Miss Kimura to the hatch leading to the *Bordeaux*. Captain Mori-

ta and the Lady Takagi were just ahead of them.

The great Lady Takagi stepped through into the docking tunnel without a backward glance. The captain followed.

"Miss Kimura?" Osiris called softly as the younger woman seemed to pause briefly at the hatch.

She turned in his direction, her head tilted downwards, her gaze still averted.

"Yes, Lieutenant?"

"Safe journey, Miss Kimura. Perhaps our paths might cross again one day."

Her head bowed lower. "I would not object to such a day."

Now what does that mean? he thought.

Osiris turned to face the central corridor of the *Masuyo*.

"Rina," her soft voice sounded behind him.

Osiris turned.

Her head was held high, and her dark eyes met his own.

"My name," she said simply, "is Rina."

Osiris felt his chest rise as he inhaled sharply.

"My name's Osiris," he managed to gasp out.

"Safe journey, Osiris," she said.

"Safe journey, Rina," he responded.

She turned, stepped through the hatch, and made her way to the waiting *Bordeaux*.

Wonder if I can get a transfer to Callisto Base? he pondered.

Inspired by the authors of the 1930s-1960s, Spencer E. Hart's goal is to "write adventure stories with a touch of romance and moral order." He can be contacted via his blog at spencerhartwriting.wordpress.com"

The Best Workout

By FREDERICK GERO HEIMBACH

Cedric is promised the experience of a lifetime from a new high-tech gym facility: a full-body virtual workout that promises to give you all of the action, excitement, and adventure of the pulps! But is it okay to enjoy all that the pulps had to offer?!

"So, about this workout," Cedric said. He was looking over at Clayton while he drove the car to the gym. It was hard to see Clayton's face in the pre-dawn light, but Cedric wanted badly to read his expression, to see if the enthusiasm was there, to know how he stood with him.

"Um, you—" Clayton pointed at something through the windshield. "Brakes!"

Cedric shifted his focus. The brake lights of the too-close car ahead gave the fog pretty but terrifying cherry-colored auras.

"Whoa!" Cedric braked hard. His heart pounded. *Getting my cardio in early.*

"I guess you'll just have to experience it for yourself," Clayton replied, remembering the question. He spoke guardedly. Cedric did not expect guardedly. Cedric did not *want* guardedly.

Where's that excitement I heard yesterday?

Cedric was determined to make this friendship work. He had started a new IT job and had found the office populated by young, dull software nerds and old, burned-out sales guys. Taciturn whites and Asians, all of them. Cedric was different, an extrovert, an optimist. A *brother.*

Cedric wanted Clayton to be an exception. He was also in IT, so Cedric would be working with him closely. Clayton seemed to be a genuine guy. Cedric wanted not to detect in him the guardedness some whites show around African Americans.

Some people, it's like they think you're keeping score.

"Come on, man," Cedric said. "Give me details. How good is it? How real does it feel?"

"Don't worry about that. It's really real."

"That's the point, right? It's so good, the workout isn't even a workout?"

The fog was turning into misty rain. Despite the crap visibility, Cedric risked another look at Clayton. He gave him a "come on, buddy" smile. Clayton hesitated, then shrugged.

"To be honest, yeah: it's the best workout ever," Clayton spoke low and relaxed. "I go four times a week, and it's almost like it's not enough."

Clayton's voice got even softer. "It's an *addiction.*" He laughed, abruptly. It was a very white laugh, but warm.

There it is. He's coming around.

"No, it's not an addiction," Clayton corrected. "Or, well, a small one. But not too much."

That white laugh again.

"I guess I know what you mean." Cedric didn't, not nearly enough.

"I *love* it," Clayton kept on, showing the same intensity when Cedric had overheard him telling George about it in the "developer's bullpen," which was really just a collection of low-walled cubicles in the corner of the big room. Cedric had emerged from a hall and there was Clayton, bearded but neatly so, talking to George, a programmer with, honestly, a weird personality; he was a nail-biter in a stained tee shirt, and his sweat tended to puddle on the spot where his inward-caving sternum met his outward-bulging gut.

The two had been talking low, conspiratorially, and Clayton's eyes were lively as he was talking up "the challenges of the scenario" and "a particularly edgy narrative" at "the new gym." Cedric had seen exercise evangelism before—heck, he had *done* exercise evangelism before—but this was something different. Something more.

As soon as Clayton noticed Cedric, they had fallen silent. Cedric asked Clayton about it later, but Clayton had been shy. Cedric persisted, though, so here they were, going to the mysterious gym together.

Clayton was still talking. "It's like nothing else. But I guess I better shut up. 'Cause if I over-hype it—"

"Yeah. Don't want to—"

"You'll find out for yourself, soon enough."

"You talked about 'narrative.' You said

it was like pulp fiction—"

"Exactly. It's exactly like that."

"I loved adventure stories, growing up. Doc Savage—"

"You're a Doc Savage fan? And Conan?"

"Conan, *Princess of Mars*, definitely. All those naked Martians."

Cedric joined his percussive laugh with Clayton's warm laugh. It felt good.

"Wait! Turn there." Clayton pointed. "Here. Turn!"

Cedric slammed on his brakes for the second time. He would have never guessed this was the place.

Cedric had expected a storefront in a strip mall. This was a deep parking lot crisscrossed with green dotted lines, weeds marking the many cracks in the asphalt. At the lot's perimeter stood a few warehouses—or was that humble word too grandiose for those unpainted lumber shacks slouching in the hazy dawn light?

This is so seedy.

Clayton continued to direct Cedric, waving him toward the back of the lot and twirling his finger so they would go behind a cinder block building. The entrance was out of sight around the corner.

The modest sign over the door said: *Primeval Combat Club.*

They paid the employee at the front desk and got their booth assignments. The facility was supposed to be cutting edge and yet the acrylic diffusers hanging on the strobing fluorescent lights were yellow with age. Clayton pointed to them. "Don't worry. They invested their money where it counts."

Clayton's booth was past Cedric's. Cedric

opened the door with his number. He paused.

"Dive right in," Clayton said, glancing back. "The interface is completely intuitive."

"Yeah, good, I'll figure it out," said Cedric, not as confident as his words.

"You got this." Clayton's laugh was cut off completely as Cedric pulled the door shut.

In the tomb-like quiet, Cedric tossed his bag on the floor and removed his track pants. He stepped up onto the platform, a raised circle with a treadmill built into it. Above him hung an encircling array of mechanical arms, poised like the legs of a hungry black widow. Cedric slipped into the one-piece the clerk had given him. Clayton, a regular, owned his own personal suit, and Cedric found out why: although they laundered the suits after each use, a faint funky odor emanated from this one, mark of the previous user—a scent of panic no detergent had been quite able to wash away.

Cedric closed the zipper. The suit woke with a twinkle of lights at the elbows and knees. There was little more to do but don the special gloves and boots, plus a helmet to cover his head, including his face. While his vision was blocked, something gently jostled various parts of his body. He decided it must be the black widow taking hold of his suit at its various contact points. If so, the machine was remarkably gentle and precise.

Well, it better be. I'm supposed to forget it's even there.

The helmet's internal display lit up grad-ually. A start button appeared. As Cedric raised his right hand, a generic, cartoonish (and Caucasian) hand moved in concert. Guided by Cedric, the virtual hand pressed the start button.

A list of vital statistics appeared. Everything appeared either correct (height: 5 foot 11 inches; weight: 178 pounds; age 28; race/ethnicity: West African) or plausible (BMI: 24.8, heart rate 68 bpm). Cedric did not need the *Edit* button and so clicked *Accept.*

Why does it care about my race? Cedric wondered.

Now came the choices. A menu titled *Adventure Genre* appeared. The following list included *Superhero, Explorer/Adventurer, Astronaut/Sci-Fi, Epic Fantasy, Horror/Ghost Hunter, Pirate, Police Investigation,* and *Warrior.* Cedric's virtual finger pressed *Explorer/Adventurer.*

The next menu was *Environment.* From the choices of *Jungle, Desert, Arctic, Industrial Complex, Mountain, Ship at Sea, Urban Apocalypse, Underwater, Rooftops, Dockyard,* Cedric chose *Jungle.*

Next came time period. Cedric passed over *Futuristic, Present, Victorian, Napoleonic, Renaissance, Dark Ages, Classical,* and *Bronze Age* and clicked *Primitive.*

For continent, Cedric's sense of loyalty guided him to *Africa.*

The next two menus had choices analogous to movie ratings. For *Violence,* Cedric chose *R.* A certain first-time shyness (plus the fear of being watched, although confidentiality was guaranteed) made him choose *PG* for *Sexuality.*

The next rating confused him: *Racialist Content*. Inside the helmet, Cedric scowled. *Isn't "racialist" just a euphemism for "racist"?*

Cedric chose *General Audiences*.

The next menu was titled *Effort Level*. Cedric decided against *Extreme*, but he was a fit guy. He touched the next choice down: *Extra Intense*.

The screen went dark. The only thing visible was a familiar gear icon in the upper-right edge of his vision for menu access. A theatrical rumble, too low for his ears but felt deep in his loins, gave Cedric a thrill of anticipation.

A faint orange light registered upon Cedric's retinas. A wind from nowhere enveloped him with an uncomfortably warm humidity. He smelled something earthy. The light brightened into a region with a straight border below and a long fade up: a horizon. A pinprick blaze, too bright for any color, stabbed his eyes as a reedy pipe played a three-note motif. Cedric blinked. Vertical interruptions in the bright region resolved into silhouettes of trees. Cedric was watching an equatorial African sunrise.

The trees were exotic, not really deciduous but certainly not evergreen. The branches ended with broad fronds like palm trees but the smooth trunks branched into fractals of boughs and branches. They were perfect for climbing. Too perfect.

Cedric looked around. He knew mechanical sensors must be hooked into his helmet to monitor his movements, but his neck muscles felt no resistance. He saw himself among a group of grass huts. On the ground a few steps away was a smoldering campfire.

The light was bright enough to see everything clearly now. Beyond some trees to the right stood timeworn columns and a lintel. They formed the entrance of a pyramidal temple of graven stone. In the foreground ahead stood a construction of lashed bamboo (Bamboo? This was supposed to be Africa) that might have been a lookout tower or a gibbet. Beyond were trees, then a beach. To the left was a steep rock slope that terminated at a wide flat top.

Cedric regarded the rock. It was rough, with knobby protrusions at regular intervals—conveniently regular. Cedric loved rock climbing. He decided to explore the high ground.

As Cedric walked, he knew the treadmill must be moving under his feet. The hi-fi virtual world hid that reality well. It told him he arrived at the cliff and touched the rock face, and he believed it. The faceted rock dug into his palm as he began to climb. It was Cedric's glove that poked his palm and a mechanical arm that provided resistance as he pulled himself up: straightforward haptics. But Cedric quickly forgot about all that. This African jungle was the real deal.

Cedric climbed. The wall was a hundred feet high in his estimation. He felt his muscles warm to the effort, lats and delts, rhomboids, biceps, and quads. A light breeze picked up, just enough for comfort. This felt like a good, general workout—but nothing "extra intense" and certainly nothing worthy of Clayton's hype.

A third of the way up, Cedric looked over his shoulder to take in the view. Everything looked gorgeous—sharp and intensely green. His eyes passed over the abandoned village below. A movement of something tawny and predatory caught his eye. The not-quite-familiar creature was ambling with an insouciant grace into the clearing Cedric had just vacated.

What…the…?

Some unseen musician began beating a big drum.

The animal sniffed the ground, trotted to the wall, and looked up. Two saber fangs glinted in the low angled sun. The creature—a tiger on steroids—caught sight of him and roared.

The sound, artificially reverberant, sent a shockwave of fear through Cedric's torso and right down into his nuts.

The animal's paws were unnaturally prehensile, and it began climbing the cliff. Its eyes bored into Cedric's. The creature was hulking and hungry and comprehensively badass.

Oh shit.

Cedric climbed for his life. The logical part of his brain—the part up high, or in front, or wherever—told Cedric the saber-toothed tiger coming up from below was merely a projection onto a screen, and the ache in his muscles was the result of resistance from a set of haptic levers, and that he was standing on a platform one foot above the floor in his exercise booth, not forty to fifty feet above the floor of an African jungle in the year fifty thousand (or million) B.C.

Cedric's lizard brain—the part that skulked low and apprehensive in the bottom of his skull—was unpersuaded by Cedric's logical brain. It ordered his adrenal gland to squirt *red alert*-levels of hormonal fear into his bloodstream. The weariness in his arms faded as he climbed like never before. The jagged rock tore into his palms and soles. He wondered, in that logical part of his brain that was being given less and less to do, whether he would come out of this workout with bloody hands.

Another roar rattled his eardrums. Cedric noticed more drums were playing, and their tempo was quickening. A whiff of musk that said "huge male predator" filled his nose. The big cat was just below him. Cedric wondered if he would come out of this workout alive.

The cat struck Cedric's leg with a paw the size of a catcher's mitt. Cedric's right hand was torn from the rock and he swung to the left, hanging from one arm. The tiger's next swing missed him. The animal's musk combined with Cedric's own fear-infused body odor in a dizzying bouquet. The tiger's saber teeth, two ivory spears, were inches from Cedric's feet. He snatched desperately for another handhold.

The rock cliff was cracked and crumbly. A piece of it broke off as Cedric pulled on it. Taking a trajectory he did not expect, the loose rock arced straight toward the tiger's face. At the same moment, the tiger's mouth opened wide for another roar.

Nothing but net! The falling rock dropped into the exact center of the great cat's maw and lodged deep in its throat.

The animal gagged and shook its head in panic. It huffed, but the rock was stuck fast.

The tiger, convulsing, jerked back. Four paws scrabbled desperately. The animal's body raised up and balanced on one hind leg—then gravity asserted itself. The tiger pivoted backwards with a tragic, balletic tumble and then it bounced its way downward. Each blow against the rocky incline splattered increasing amounts of blood. Unseen brazen trumpets blared a minor chord.

Although the tiger's downfall was spellbinding, Cedric could not help noticing a small tawny spot, a miniature version of the tiger, scamper across the village clearing to the rock wall just as the tiger's plunge reached its end. The tiger kitten, with the heedlessness of a newborn, ran right into the shadow of its sire just in time to be crushed by the shattering collision.

Cedric heard the revolting crunch as father and child died together. A red streak down the side of the cliff drew a dashed line pointed at the disaster, and he could not look away.

Cedric noticed his breathing and the ache in his right arm. He had hung by one hand as he had watched. He turned to get a two-handed grip.

Cedric heard another roar. This one was distant, but full of rage. Another streak of tawny feline power crossed the clearing below. The second tiger—mate and mother of the dead!—beheld the disaster, then looked up to find the murderer.

Her eyes blazed with vengeance. She began to climb.

The drummers resumed their slow beat. The sun's heat intensified. The wind bore the scent of blood.

No time to rest.

Cedric climbed with renewed energy. Repeated roars gave him all the information he needed about the tiger's closing distance. His head-start was better than before, but Cedric was not sure how he could beat the cat to the top.

With the tiger now just feet away, Cedric arrived at a small ledge. Several loose rocks the size of his head sat there.

Giving me a fighting chance, Cedric's neglected logical brain told him.

Without a backwards glance, Cedric flipped one rock off the ledge with his left hand. He flipped another with his right. Cedric heard an outraged roar and the now familiar sound of paws scraping rock. Cedric continued to climb, and a good thing, too—another roar told him the cat had not backslid far. She would close upon him fast.

More decent-sized boulders appeared on conveniently-spaced ledges. *Too obvious,* Cedric's brain told him. *It takes me out of the narrative. They should do better than this.* Cedric used the boulders to make the tiger dodge and backslide even as he made more progress upward.

And then, before he knew it, Cedric was pulling himself up onto a spreading meadow of tall grass. *Mesa. Savanna. Whatever.* Cedric's chatty logical brain was unsure of the right word and struggling to stay relevant.

Cedric's aching arms got a break as his running muscles, quads, glutes, and hamstrings, broke into a full sprint.

Grass as high as his armpits stretched before him for hundreds of yards. The tree line encircling this meadow was unobtainable, assuming the tiger came over the lip of the cliff soon.

An exultant roar told him she was doing just that.

Before him were two choices. The scenario made it quite clear those were the only two. Fifty yards away stood a tall tree—impossibly tall, and spindly straight. Next to it was an equally tall shaft of rock, roughly square in cross-section and about four times the thickness of the tree.

The vine-covered tree had small branches evenly spaced: a ladder in all but name. The rock shaft was climber-friendly like the cliff, but with straighter sides. The cat might not be able to negotiate the rock.

Cedric sprinted to the rock.

Once again, the timing benefited Cedric—just barely. He lifted himself with tired arms above the ground. He felt hot, muggy air swish about his feet as the tiger's teeth snapped shut just an inch below his bare foot.

The tiger was nothing if not adaptable. As Cedric clung, panting, two dozen feet above the ground, the prehistoric tiger bounded to the adjacent tree. Her claws had no trouble finding purchase on its bark.

Shit. Shit. No rest.

With lungs hungry for oxygen, Cedric climbed again, but in moments the tiger was above him. Cedric moved laterally—and did so just in time. The tiger lunged at him across the several-yard gap. From the far side of the rock, Cedric watched the tiger scrape uselessly on the rocky surface and fall to the ground.

The animal was unhurt and immediately began climbing the tree again. Cedric wanted to rest in his seemingly secure position on the far side of the rock, but the surface there was weirdly friable. Already he could feel the clay-like material disintegrating in his hands.

Cedric, too, fell to the ground.

The jolt to his legs, his loss of balance, the blow all along his torso, arm, and shoulder—they all felt real. The haptics did their job.

Okay, not quite. Cedric was sore, but his logical brain complained the fall should have broken his legs. That complaint was silenced when the big cat leaped from her spot high on the tree and landed next to Cedric.

Cedric ran around the rock as the tiger chased him. Abandoning the rock as useless, Cedric exercised his only remaining option and climbed the tree.

This was the better choice. The branches were perfectly spaced so the tiger, faster in the open, could not keep pace with Cedric. Man and animal snaked and weaved their way among the branches that alternated north-south with east-west, and Cedric built up a lead.

Cedric was no longer racing for his life, but the tiger was not tiring. They climbed and climbed. No plan formed in Cedric's logical brain for what to do when the branches ran out.

Cedric ran out of rock first. The tree, a freak of nature, was taller than the rocky spindle. Cedric paused to take stock as the tiger caught up.

A vine hung nearby. The scenario practically begged Cedric to pull a Tarzan and swing over to the rock. *Me, Tarzan*: this thought prompted Cedric's curiosity. He looked down at himself and noticed for the first time his dark, sweat-slick body was clothed only in a skimpy leopard loincloth. He laughed out loud.

Cedric was not sure what standing on the flat area on top of the rock would gain him. There were flattened oval rocks lying there, begging him to be used—but for what? They resembled something Cedric could not quite name. Cedric could throw them like before, but what...

Axe heads.

Cedric thought about the branches he was holding on to. They all had a characteristic shape, emerging from the trunk of the tree for about three feet, then branching into exactly two smaller, but still stout, branches like tines of tuning forks.

Axe heads. Vines. Handles. Cedric's logic brain proudly put it all together.

Cedric yanked a branch. It broke off conveniently, right at the trunk. He bit off a section of vine. (The haptics had trouble making that feel right, and the taste was definitely wrong.) He held the vine and branch in his mouth like a dog and swung on another vine, pendulum style, pushing himself off the trunk to build momentum until it was enough to fling him down to the rock.

The tiger's arrival just then gave him the will to let go.

Again, Cedric's adrenaline squirter squirted. He arced through the air. The virtual reality machine simulated the momentum of the arc. The virtual height was genuinely terrifying.

Cedric landed on the rock's top. He slid, but his grasping hands stopped him. He was safe.

The tiger was not happy. She roared out her wrath. Her eyes stared pure hatred at him.

Cedric did not pause. He trimmed his branch to a convenient length and wedged one of the oval stones into the Y. He wrapped the vine around the stone in a crisscross pattern like a canonical Indian's tomahawk.

Cedric lifted the axe to test its heft. The tiger, having paced about to find the best jumping point, coiled to spring.

Cedric would have only one shot at this.

The tiger leaped. Cedric swung the axe. He hoped his vine's knot was boy scout-reliable.

The stone axe head met the side of the tiger's head midflight. The impact jarred Cedric's arms. The tiger's eyes crossed as the impact passed from skull to brain.

Cedric stepped aside and let the unconscious tiger sail past him and down to her death.

The world faded to black, and once again, that Spielbergesque movie soundtrack swelled in Cedric's helmet.

Cedric caught his breath. He felt a gratifying ache in every muscle of his body.

Three Minute Rest announced the UI in pale yellow letters. It asked, *Would you like to change your settings?*

Cedric, still panting, clicked *Yes.*

On a whim, he changed the time period to *Victorian* and bumped the *Sexuality* up a notch to *PG-13*. He hesitated, then changed *Racialist Content* way up to *Restricted*. Out of curiosity.

This'll be interesting, Cedric thought. Seconds ticked off. He remembered the helmet had a water tube and took a deep swig. The water was warm and tasted like plastic.

The full light of noon came up on another African village. Before Cedric could get a good look, a woman's shriek grabbed his attention.

He pivoted his head to get a sense of the sound's direction. *There!* It came from over a low hill to his left. Cedric took off running. The woman's renewed screams drove him on.

At the crest of the hill he saw her. She was in a wagon with iron bars, like one for transporting circus animals. She was further restrained by ropes holding her wrists aloft. The wagon was drawn along a dirt path by a pair of horses. Cedric could not see the driver.

As he drew near, Cedric noticed the woman had skin just as dark as his. Her perfectly proportioned body was covered—just barely—by an animal skin dress. *That leopard print again!* She wore a necklace of lion's teeth on a chain of gold and her glossy black hair was held high by a cylinder of delicate gold filigree. Her cheekbones, bright eyes, and red mouth projected youthful vigor. Her eyes flashed with regal outrage. She was movie-star beautiful.

And right now she needed a strong man to save her.

Cedric bellowed in rage. The horses were reined to a stop. The driver and his partner jumped off the wagon.

The men—slave traders, clearly—were straight out of the world of Sir Richard Francis Burton. The pith helmets they wore had not protected their pale faces from sunburn. They wore ridiculous sideburn whiskers of strawberry blond, and—leaving no cliché unturned—each man wore a monocle. Khaki uniforms, cargo shorts, and argyle knee socks in thick wool completed the look.

The driver unsheathed a wicked Bowie knife and charged straight for Cedric.

Unarmed, Cedric could do little but dodge. He wondered exactly how the haptics would behave if he gave the slaver a chance to stick his knife in. He decided he would make sure he did not find out.

The woman had paused her screaming to watch the battle, but now she resumed. Cedric risked a glance and saw the second man had entered the cage and was running his filthy hands over her barely clothed body. Cedric did not have the luxury of caution.

He looked back to his opponent and barely dodged the next lunge. The man was too fast to disarm barehanded, so Cedric looked around for a makeshift weapon. Seeing nothing on the path, he ran into the tall grass. The woman's screams became more urgent, and his opponent simply waited on the path, taunting him in something that sounded like Dutch.

Cedric circled around him to climb onto the wagon. A six-foot iron bar came free in his hand.

Without hesitation, he swung it at his opponent. The man's hat and skull crumpled under its weight in a crimson display.

That felt good.

But the second white man had torn his own bar from the wagon now and was upon him. They fought with the bars, kung fu style, neither gaining the advantage. Cedric began to tire, but as he did, another white man—another ugly, bemonocled, sunburned, colonial stereotype—emerged from the tall grass and climbed into the wagon. The woman renewed her screams as Colonel Blimp No. 3 picked up where his comrade had left off, fondling the woman.

This is pissing me off.

Cedric redoubled his efforts. Despite his aching arms, he hooked his opponent's leg with the end of his bar. The man went down and his bar went whirling into the grass. Cedric kneeled down to teach the slaver a bare-knuckled lesson.

The monocle made a convenient bull's eye. Cedric felt the glass shatter under his fist as he pounded it repeatedly. Blood, mixed with clear fluid, ran from the eye socket.

As long as he still struggled, Cedric pounded the slaver's face with a wrath of unaccustomed righteousness. It felt really, really, really good.

When the man went limp, Cedric turned his attention to Chester the Molester in the cage. The man turned to him with a drawn machete, and they set to combat.

Another slaver walked in out of the grass and climbed into the cage.

This pattern went on. As each fighter was killed, he would be replaced by the happy-hands in the cage, who was in turn replaced by another white slaver coming out of the grass. The idiots never ganged up on Cedric, but there seemed to be a limitless supply of them. The beautiful African princess never tired of screaming, and although her abusers tore at her skimpy clothes, they never quite came off.

Through it all, Cedric's heart pounded and his muscles ached and his nose inhaled an aerosol of sweat and blood and he had a rip-roaring blast—but he never quite forgot the computer was playing his emotions like a fiddle.

Cedric faced more machetes, Bowie knives, and bars torn from the wagon, plus rifles used only as clubs (apparently these slavers were too stupid to buy ammo) and whips. In response, he made his own whip from the horses' harness. That, in turn, gave him an idea to exit the scenario.

He stopped killing the men. Instead, he stunned the two current opponents with measured punches to their faces. As they were still conscious, though groggy, no replacements came out of the tall grass. In a scene worthy of the cheesiest pulp fiction, and to the swelling accompaniment of an invisible orchestra, he cut the woman's bonds and the other horse's harness with a discarded Bowie knife. Together they rode bareback on their liberated mounts down the path and into the sunset, but not before Cedric's whip gave the two remaining slavers a souvenir: a red gash across their ugly, sunburned cheeks.

The sun sank unnaturally fast, the final

Need Fantasy or Sci-fi Art?

Commercial Rights
Included for:
* Illustrations
* Book Cover Art
* Fantasy Maps
* Logos and more

OtherRealmStudio.com

Paula Richey
Custom Art & Illustration Services

orchestral chords faded like John Williams having a bad day, and the screen went dark. A profound satisfaction unlike anything he could remember came over Cedric—a satisfaction tainted by the expectation his logical brain would eventually have something disapproving to say.

The computer displayed the elapsed time: *65 minutes.*

65 minutes!

It was past time to leave. Cedric powered down and unhooked and emerged from his cubicle.

Sweaty Clayton was waiting for him with a grin. "Well?"

"Oh, yeah," Cedric said as he wiped his brow with a towel. "You were right. It was everything you said it would be. I mean—wow!"

They entered the locker room and Cedric peeled the suit off his body. The cool air felt brisk against his exposed limbs. Judging by Clayton's glistening skin and shy little smile, he too had been taken for quite a ride.

"What time period did you pick?" asked Cedric as they relaxed under the showers.

"Classical. You know, togas and Emperors. You?"

"Primitive, then Victorian."

"Heh. Those are good ones."

"The hand to hand combat was...was..."

Cedric was grasping for an adequate superlative. Clayton gave him no help.

"...well, I guess they call it *primeval* for a reason! To feel my fist pounding those guys—"

Clayton nodded.

"And I found out, if you boost the sex

A New World Requires Clear Vision

Dr. Michael Chase,
Visionary

"The SETI radio-telescopes are looking in the wrong place. It's not 'Out There' that we will find our spiritual peers in the universe, it is inside our own minds.

"First Contact isn't some science fiction future, it is happening right now, all around us.

"The spiritual upheavals in America today are the growing pains of a new form of life, one that combines Earthly and Stellar intelligence.."

--Dr. Michael Chase,
Mankind's Eternal Odyssey
**Clear Vision Ministries,
Pasadena, CA, 1972.**

score, you get to save a gorgeous woman."

"Yeah." Clayton shut off the water and gave his full attention to drying off. Why was he so quiet?

"I mean," continued Cedric, speaking just a little faster, "I didn't bump it up *too* far. I can only imagine what might happen if you went real high."

"Yeah," said Clayton awkwardly.
Shit. Change the subject.
"And that so-called *racialism*—"
Clayton may have been technically na-

ked, technically standing there without a stitch of clothing, but it was like he had donned multiple suits of armor. His face had gone rigid, turned into a dead, plastic thing like the mask Michael Myers wore in *Halloween.*

"Oh," mumbled Clayton, "*racialism.*"

"So, you—"

"No," said Clayton, looking at something over *there.* "I never. Tried that."

"Ah. Yeah. I mean, me neither."

"I mean, why go there?"

"Yeah. I wondered. You know, purely out of curiosity. But that would be...would be..."

"Exactly."

Cedric and Clayton dressed. They rode to the office in silence. They did their jobs.

Subsequently, Cedric became a regular at the Primeval Combat Club, but he always went alone, and Clayton did not mention it again. They never quite hit it off, although they were always perfectly polite.

Frederick Gero Heimbach lives a pulp fiction life and takes notes. His family lives with him, warily, in Ann Arbor, Michigan. His first novel is The Devil's Dictum, about an absurd alt-history United States founded by Satan-worshiping pirates.

A Song in Deepest Darkness

By JASON RAY CARNEY

Pardew and Bellik sacrificed much to discover the true name of their god, the Hearthfather! Bellik's death places the solution out of his brother's reach, but the sorcerer Ka promises that a necromantic artifact will aid in retrieving the answers!

Spitting bloody foam, Bellik died before he could tell the secret name to Pardew. What dark insight had Bellik derived from the allegories and symbols told in verse in the many codices, scrolls, cryptolects, and annals he had studied? The brothers had traveled far and wide, to the Great Harbor at Ouon, to Fuor of the Golden Palace, to Re of the Thirty Silver-faced Lords, and all for the sake of finding any hint, any whisper, of the enigma's resolution: the long-lost true name of their brotherhood's godlet, whom they called the "Hearthfather."

The Hearthfather's true name, the annalists reported and metaphysicians surmised, was a word of power that could work many miracles: break fevers, restore wholeness to lepers, exorcise demons, and resurrect the dead. The wonders attributed to the name were numerous, and the agony the brotherhood felt for being ignorant of it was depthless. And in the course of their quest to recover it, Bellik had paid for his insight: he had been murdered, thrice shanked in a

dark alley by a masked cultist's poignard—red retribution for stealing a glance of a cipher carved on a triangular tablet of iron hung by silver wire over a vat of acid in the deepest octagonal sanctum of a temple consecrated to a nameless devil. It was through Pardew's clever working of pauper's sorcery that they penetrated the vault. When their intrusion had been discovered, the triangular tablet was swiftly destroyed, released into the acid—but not before Bellik's pupils dilated to pinpoints and he hissed, "I understand now."

Though they had been able to find egress down a dark, trash-strewn alley of scampering rats, one cultist had followed and struck. Pardew had not been able to slay in retribution the fast-footed cultist, whose grisly work had left him with his brother bleeding in his arms. Cradling him, tears flowing into his beard, he saw his brother's hooded eyes, porcelain-pale skin, and blue lips, and thought him dead. But a spark of life lingered.

"The Hearthfather's name? Please tell

me, brother!" Pardew sobbed. With a trembling hand and the help of his brother, Bellik scrawled an enigma on a scrap of parchment using his own blood: annotating a triangle were three bizarre ideograms unknown to Pardew. And with his fading breath, with tears in his bloodshot eyes, Bellik tried to whisper final words, but croaking, died, leaving Pardew and their order's ignorance intact. Later, Pardew took the scrap of parchment adorned with a secret name written in blood, rolled it into a tiny scroll, and secreted it away in a latched triangular amulet of iron that he wore around his neck.

Long had Pardew ruminated on those cryptic ideograms, tried and failed to understand and translate them. In deep mourning, often moved to tears of sadness and rage, he haunted the cluttered library of his order's fortress, grew gaunt of face and thin-armed. His eyes strained and several candles melted as he read and re-read and annotated his brother's massive black-boarded portfolio of notes, diaries, scrawled diagrams, and ciphers, but the ideograms that hung at his neck stubbornly refused to yield up their lucre. Try as he might, Pardew could find no principle to tie it all together to wrest the appellation of their godlet from the grasp of mystery. Though Bellik had often shared his wild speculations over ale with Pardew, his reading and studies ran deeper than his brother could follow with his lesser brain, into labyrinths and grottos of history, philosophy, metaphysics, and theology.

Bereft of his brother's guidance, Pardew, the one-time holy man, drifted into ennui and sensuous indulgence. For months he haunted alehouses and smoking dens of ill-repute and sought distraction in dicing, cards, and the unloving caresses of lithe bodies bought for coin. Alas, he could not find forgetfulness there, and the ideograms inked in blood that he grasped tightly as he restless slept haunted him. The secret of his godlet's name gnawed at him, and he missed his brother sorely. And so, after one particularly indulgent bender where he awoke disgusted by his profligacy, he vowed to his dead brother's shade he would take up the quest again. After several months, his beard, streaked with white, was as long as Bellik's had been, and now two blades hung sheathed at his hip.

It was in the dusty city of Nool in the northern stretches of the Demesne of Mogal that Pardew came upon the thin warlock, Ka, once of Dis-Penethor. The pale, dark-eyed, shaved-headed sorcerer smelled too much of garlic and onions, and his red robes were sewn with stars of silver, sigils of his unspeakable dishonor. His triangle-cut black beard and vertical-iris sorcerer's eyes affected a bizarre figure who seemed possessed of forbidden, depthless knowledge. By the flickering light of a single tallow candle over a plate of marinated mushrooms, leeks, and dog's meat, the sorcerer and the bearded monk compared notes and spoors and discussed other worlds:

"By this portfolio I see your brother's shadowy mind is a maze, terrible but suggestive, and there is much here that correlates with my own inquiries, but, alas, the Hearthfather's name flits just beyond the range of this study," Ka said, his voice like water hissing on coals. He caressed Bellik's black-boarded portfolio with a knotty and many-ringed hand.

"How do I know you're speaking truth?" asked Pardew, his eyes narrowing with suspicion. He sipped his drinking jack brimming with red wine and stroked his beard. "Sorcerers are not eager to share their secrets, it is said."

"True, true, but we may be of value to each other, perhaps," responded Ka consolingly. "There are several variables here that are opaque to me, riddles and enigmas that are ciphered by your brother's suspicions. I could do more if we could summon your brother's shade and put questions to him. Oh, what strange doors of insight we might pry open! What weird windows we might gaze through!"

Pardew's hackles raised. His hand went unbidden to the amulet that hung hidden in his robes. "You can summon poor Bellik's spirit?" he asked. "You are possessed of such a power?"

Ka scoffed. "Do not be so impressed, holy man! Usually, yes," he said. "Had I but a single gravelight candle, all would be at our ease, but the reagent to create such an artifact, the churned fat of an infant child, is difficult to procure and abominable. Luckily, however, the trick that can be done in several other ways. Spiritspeaking is a useful art common among my cadres, but it is beyond my skill at present, beset as I am by poverty."

Pardew narrowed his eyes again. "You must know I have some coin to spare. Though my brotherhood is not overly rich, we are not close-fisted. But we are weary of mountebanks who might take advantage of our generosity with false promises. How much do you need?"

Ka scoffed again. "Do not worry, holy man. As far as coin is concerned, we need more than you or your brothers have, unfortunately," he hissed languorously. "Such a device as I have in mind, a toy to most sorcerers, would come at a crown's price, and only if one could be found at market."

"Hellfire!" Pardew belched. "Then my brother's secret died with him!" He put his face in his hands and sighed deeply. "Another flagon of black bitter for me this night, it seems," he said.

Ka gazed at Pardew over his chalice of red wine and through a screen of purple smoke snaking from the man's crackling seed pipe; what seemed like blood glistened on his thin lips. "You surrender easily, Brother Pardew," he said, his yellow, fang-like teeth gleaming. "Indeed, although we cannot purchase the device like a sack of roots at market, we might—" and here he licked his lips and narrowed his serpent's eyes. "—*procure* what we need in other ways."

Pardew felt the shadow feeling and the lights seemed to dim; the air became conspiratorial. He leaned forward, hands folded.

"Tell me," whispered Pardew. He unbuckled the two blades that hung sheathed at his hip and laid them on the table, a gesture pregnant with meaning; their silvery pommels and hilts glimmered in the candle's light.

In a hushed, skullduggering voice, Ka told of the Howling Furnace, the former underground fastness of Shelvox the Black, a long-missing necromancer of legend, and his Singing Jorum, an ancient bell-bowl that compelled spirits who had secrets to speak. "With the Singing Jorum, we might get your brother to speak. But hearken to the risk: though Shelvox was dragged down to other worlds by shadowy hands long ago, his Howling Furnace is yet a dangerous place, for its lowest cellars connect to a deeper darkness that is haunted by creatures who have never known the light. Only a soft-padded shadow might stand a chance. Through arduous study, I have been able to render maps of the Furnace and can approximate the chamber where the Singing Jorum can be found. I would trade my secrets for your courage and blade."

"*Blades*," corrected Pardew in hushed tones. "I have two of them."

"Then we must discuss our conditions," whispered Ka. "I shall provide the map, and if we succeed in procuring the Singing Jorum, I will try to summon your brother's spirit."

"And in return?" asked Pardew.

Ka placed three long and taloned fingers on his pursed lips: "First, I shall keep the Singing Jorum for my own. It has uses beyond spiritspeaking."

Pardew nodded.

"Second, you shall gift to me your brother's portfolio. It treats much more than the lost name of your Hearthfather, and given enough time to study it, it might bear strange fruit."

Pardew flared his nostrils. "You ask a lot. That would be a sore loss. My brother devoted his life, and lost it redly, in the gathering of those whispers."

Ka lovingly caressed the black-boarded portfolio. "Very well," he sighed. "I had hoped to aid in your order's restoration—"

"Have those scraps, then," Pardew grunted. "Bellik was no scholar for knowledge's sake. His one goal was to call upon the Hearthfather using his true name."

Ka grinned and steepled his fingers. "Then, to my final condition."

"Go on," said Pardew.

"When you learn the secret name of the Hearthfather, I, too, shall share in that knowledge."

Pardew gasped at the sorcerer's brazen demand: "Never!" he said, bolting upright, knocking over his jack of wine, and throwing on his cloak and hood indignantly. He dropped two coins to the table, turned to go, and nearly toppled a shrieking scullery maid bearing a jug of beer.

"Wait!" hissed Ka. "Please!"

Pardew turned, red-faced in anger: "If ever my brotherhood learns the Hearthfather's name, then that secret will be protected as our most sacred mystery, and only the most devout will learn it, and only after they find favor in our Lord's eyes."

Ka held up one finger: "Very well. I admire your loyalty, faith, and adherence to principle, holy man. What, then, can you propose as a substitute of equal value?"

Pardew gazed into the sorcerer's vertical

irises that shimmered with wine: "I have heard the gossipmongers say that necromancers have use of bodies in their truck with ghouls?"

Ka grinned, sipped his wine, inhaled purple seedsmoke from the side of his mouth, and nodded.

Pardew swallowed, and when he spoke, the odious words stuck in his throat: "My brotherhood's fortress has a tomb—" He averted his guilty eyes.

Ka produced a cylinder of black wood, its corners hasped with dull steel, its battered cap secured with a cruel lock. "The map," he said.

Pardew's breath came short. Ka's map had been true!

Shimmering on the dais was the Singing Jorum: wrought of an extramundane alloy that swirled purple, red, and black, it caught the light of Ka's staff-torch and glimmered like a living thing in the darkness.

Using the map, Pardew and Ka had navigated the maze-like laboratory-furnace of Shelvox the Black. Driven on by the prospect of secrets, they had braved this darkness for several days now, and their faces were grime-streaked and gaunt with hunger, their eyes strained by darkness and lack of sleep.

Pardew outstretched his knotty, ink-stained hand.

"Forbear! You are an overeager tom, Pardew," Ka hissed. "Let me examine the device first. Death is never far off here."

Pondering Ka's words, Pardew found himself wondering why the Singing Jorum remained here and why such a device of sorcery might be left to gather dust in this darkness. He made a fist and pulled his hand back.

The small jug of burning oil that capped Ka's staff cast dancing shadows as he wedged it between two loose flagstones. He unfolded a waxed-paper parcel containing a pair of dark goggles with lenses shaped like an insect's eyes; these he tied around his eyes. He approached the Jorum and mumbled: "We must compare these sigils to Bellik's notes."

Ka held a grease pen and opened Bellik's ponderous portfolio to a page of hieroglyphics rendered in a rough hand.

Pardew looked on, his arms crossed. "Is it safe?" he whispered.

With a frustrated sigh, Ka closed Pardew's brother's book, removed his goggles, and secreted them away in his pack. "I will not speak in ignorance," he sighed. "There may be a dangerous ward here. We must assume that Shelvox, like all sorcerers, would have jealously guarded a device such as this, but I sense no protective ward here—nothing!—and this disconcerts me."

Clapping his hands, Pardew strode past Ka and approached the Jorum. Twinkling in the flickering light, it seemed to beckon him on: *Take me, o man*, it seemed to say erotically. For the briefest of moments, Pardew thought he saw several rictus snarls floating on the Jorum's glass-like surface, and he stopped, looked around the chamber paranoically, sweat streaming down his brow.

Pardew's hand hovered over the undulating surface of the Jorum and felt heat and soft pulsing. He stood before it and gazed for several minutes upon the beautiful writing that adorned its surface and regretted that he could not read it. He leaned in to perceive its smallest filigrees that textured it. Later, after sustained scrutiny, he sat cross-legged before the dais and Jorum, the figure of a wilderness ascetic, his hands cupped on his lap.

"What shall we do?" asked Pardew. "Alas, to come this far and be cowed by ignorance and fear."

Ka sighed.

Pardew stood and swiftly picked up the object, lifted it above his head, grinning, and Ka gasped and covered his face, but nothing transpired.

Pardew smiled at his companion and turned his gaze to the Jorum: it was polished to a mirror sheen; his bearded, smiling face curved distorted across its body. It was surprisingly light and somewhat warm and swelled in luminescence as he handled it. It hummed as if it contained a small colony of bees. It was like a chunk of hot ice or frozen fire.

"Only sorcerer's work remains now, Bellik," he sighed to his brother's memory. As Pardew snugged the Jorum into his backpack, a flash of what might have been anger streaked across Ka's pinched face. Ka started to speak—

Just as he did so, however, there was a loud grinding as a stone door was pressed open. Ka looked up to see child-sized, rodent-like creatures leaping into the room, their angular knives and spearheads catching the torchlight wavering in the underground draft. The light danced on their red, waxy faces and illuminated their gaunt and hungry features.

"The doom of the Deepest Dark has come, *manlings*! *Lightdrinkers!*" said their leader in a falsetto voice like a screaming brew kettle. "Doom! Doom! *Doom!*" it shouted, relishing this word that rolled off its forked tongue.

For a moment Pardew and Ka stood there, like rooted trees, their hearts leaping to their throats, their eyes bulging, jaws dropping. A redling loosed an arrow, the head of which was forged to catch the air and scream as it sped. The bolt screeched by Pardew and snapped against the chamber wall.

"By the Hearthfather's tits!" roared Pardew.

"Fly!" cried Ka.

They bolted through an archway, taking only their backpacks but leaving Ka's staff-torch. Arrows screamed past them. Pardew's cook pot and spoon, tied to his backpack, clattered and fell as they fled. They ran down a dark thoroughfare, up spiral stairs, and through a long, tapering hallway flanked by arches shaped as teeth-filled maws and wide, circular black doorways made for non-human shapes. Redness shone in the distance, and being creatures of the sun, they hove toward the light.

Three trumpets sounded behind them, like tortured souls whistling. Flames twinkled around them like cruel eyes. The heat pressed them and drove them down the blazing path. Iron sconces forged to resemble grinning devils lined the vaulted corridor, dripped flaming pitch to the slimy stones and splashed bizarre shadows on the fungus-sprouting walls of rough-hewn brick.

Ka and Pardew stumbled into an alcove: "My staff!" Ka cursed. "It was made of a black bole of Yizdra, a rare wood, priceless and fell!" He jammed his fist in his mouth.

Sweat poured down Pardew's brow; he removed a greasy rag from his belt pouch and wiped his face. He felt the inside of his backpack for the Jorum, and when he found it, he caressed it lovingly, sighing with relief. "Thanks to the Hearthfather," he whispered. "We have it yet."

As rabbits sniffing a sleeping wolf, their curiosity had been cruelly rewarded. Beyond a bend in the snaking corridor behind them, the shrieks of devils echoed; shadows danced, and they saw the grim silhouettes of the rage-filled rabble they had bestirred.

In the distance, squeaking laughter mixed with the pattering of feet, and the trumpeting of horns carried toward them.

Pardew threw himself against the rough-hewn wall, flattened himself into shadow, and huffed deep breaths. Again, he mopped the sweat from his forehead with a rag.

Ka stood there, trembling. He wrapped his arms about his torso, then flailed them, made fists, then stamped his sandaled foot, all the while cursing incoherently in angry whispers. "Granlings!" he said, slapping his forehead. "Of course! Shelvox took granlings for thrall, and they linger here, bereft of a lord to herd them!"

The flames limned the corridor around them in a red, angry glow. Despite the shadows, they could see the corridor extended some ways into deeper darkness. They huddled here, listening intently. There was a loud clatter, the beating of several weapons on shields, and the flames and shadows seemed to press closer, to compel them deeper into the labyrinth, into the darker regions below.

"What are granlings?" Pardew asked in a whisper.

"By the black dung of Avershoust'at, the Horned One!" replied Ka. "They were humans once, most foully corrupted, shriveled by a secret art known to few; taken to thrall, they render an abominable fuel to some forbidden sorcery—hate, fear, ignorance—unto a master they are bewitched to adore. Yes, holy man, Shelvox made them that way."

Pardew grimaced. He unsheathed one of his blades. "Better to give them mercy, then," he said.

"Nay!" hissed Ka. "There are too many of the fiends for your blades. And perhaps there is a better way! As I said, the Jorum has other uses. With its calming song I might pacify these creatures. But I do not know how to make it sing just yet. Let us seek safety for now."

Pardew nodded grimly. One hand holding his blade, the other on the rough-hewn wall for guidance and balance, he pressed onward. Ka dogged his heels, occasionally stumbling. They surveyed the corridors, scanned for any familiar angle or signal to determine their location.

A corridor opened up before them, and they saw a triple-archway, a diamond-shaped atrium, and four headless statues.

Stammering, "I know this! I know this!" Ka removed the black cylinder that contained his map, unclasped it, and then unfolded a crisp, worn-edged document.

"Are we lost?" asked Pardew.

"No longer," responded Ka.

They skirted the dubious safety of the shadows and sprinted through the torchlight toward the door. The portal was a structure of ancient black boards banded with wrought iron fitted into a stone arch, the keystone of which was a grinning, three-eyed devil with flaring nostrils and curving ram's horns. Pardew reached for the thick ring fashioned for non-human hands and tugged. The door was firmly closed and did not budge.

"By the withered dugs of Ral!" Ka hissed, pushing past Pardew. He yanked the door again, and as he did so they heard a high-pitched, angry call:

"O manlings! O lightdrinkers!" sung a mellifluous voice as pale lights bobbed behind them. "Listen to how we will treat with you! We will flay you and then bind a Black Book with your skin! We will make a wine pot of your skull! We will read dark verses as your soul writhes in the chest-cage of the Horned One's breast!"

His teeth chattering, Pardew looked back and then saw them: the granlings had deep set eyes with swelling black pupils, pointed red chins, pointed red noses, and pointed red ears that tapered and stretched over round skulls. They brandished crooked spears, razorbladed chains, forking blades, and bows nocked with the black arrows that whistled and screamed like banshees. Several, perhaps twenty of them—none larger than a human child—came on laughing.

On seeing them, Pardew grabbed two handfuls of his beard, howled like an animal, and began tugging on Ka's robes. Ka knocked his grasping hands away.

"Deranged monkey!" Ka hissed. "Thou rooting, squealing hog at slaughter! Forbear! Let me be! I can save us! I can unbar this door!" He made strange gestures with his hands; the demon carving above seemed to grin at his art. His gestures completed, he shouted, "Open!"

The door groaned and budged just so, screeched as it dragged across the flagstone; the iron banding on stone made dancing sparks. The door had opened just wide enough. The light from the torches spilled into the mysterious room beyond, splashed the sharp lines of the door, and silhouetted the shapes of Pardew and Ka.

Arrows screamed shrilly; several stuck out long trains of sparks before them. The creatures screamed in cackling voices, foul to the ears.

Pressing with their backs and tired legs, Pardew and Ka pushed the door shut behind them. They stumbled deeper into yawning blackness.

From Ka's map, they had a vague idea of where they were, on a broad thoroughfare that led to a series of interconnected chambers.

Pardew ran ahead, sword flashing, his eyes slowly adjusting to the pitch darkness. Behind him Ka wheezed, holding his chest and sweating. Distantly came the ecstatic screams of the creatures, the screeching of the door, and the fierce luminescence of their red torches. This distant light brought sharp contrast to their vision, and they saw rising before them colonnades, adorned with spirals and carven eyes, that supported a many-vaulted ceiling that swelled. Several alleyways branched to left and right into deeper darkness.

They had no time to weigh this choice against that, so they issued into a random tunnel and swiftly came upon a narrow spiral stairwell. Down these stairs they ran until a chunk of stone gave way beneath Pardew's foot. He tripped, tumbled, and smashed into another door: black planks banded with iron and nail.

Standing over Pardew and gritting his teeth, Ka shoved the door with his shoulder, grunted, hissed, and spat as he tried to force it. The door gave, grinding in the brick frame.

The scent of mold and mildew issued from the ever-widening crack of the portal. Ka could not get the door completely open, but it yawned just wide enough. Ka helped Pardew to his feet before their pursuers sluiced into the chamber like slime. They slammed the door as they heard the taunts of the approaching creatures.

"Make sure the Jorum was not harmed when you stumbled," said Ka.

Pardew sighed with relief when he discovered that it was unmarred. He removed it from his backpack, and its pale light slightly illuminated the chamber. With the guidance of the Jorum's light, Pardew plied pauper's sorcery: with an egg of white chalk, he swiftly scratched a large and complex sign of warding on the door: "I oppose you with Rakefire's Resplendent Roadblock, you capering nuggets of dung!" he hissed.

Ka nodded, appreciatively. "Your folk magic is rustic but effective," he said.

For a moment they just stood there, leaning against the door, taking slow and heavy breaths, feeling their blood thrum in their temples.

Pardew sank to his knees and placed his face in his hands.

"What now, Ka? We have fared well, as far as bleating sheep before wolves go," he said, his voice thick with laughter. Ka laughed as well.

They had not completely evaded the creatures. They would surely pursue them into the labyrinth.

Pardew un-hasped his second blade—his brother's—and cradled it lovingly for a moment, admiring its simple craftsmanship. "Well, my brother, if they do find me, I swear to chop several down first. I swear they will pay a king's price for their stew meat." He kissed the blade at its cross and then re-hasped it at his hip.

Ka brought forth a bladder from his robes, took a mouthful of liquid, and passed it to Pardew. The sorcerer then unlaced a parcel and assembled a small hooded lamp;

the iron pieces clicked together snugly. He placed a lump of black grease, the last of his fuel, on the flame tray and lit it with his flint.

Light filled the large circular chamber. The rounded ceiling was supported by two arches of stone. Several embedded tiles in the ceiling formed a geometric mosaic, many eyes spiraling on a black field. The floor was mossy and uneven flagstone, ripped apart by serpent-like roots that were now dry and dead. Some mushrooms poked through the cracks, the flesh of their caps red-streaked on black. There was a round well, built of octagonal, un-grouted bricks, in the center of the room. A carpet of shaggy vegetation, a bioluminescent yellowish green fernlike growth, clung to it and undulated in the soft draft of that place. Tiny white moths fluttered around it.

Ka tied his goggles around his eyes and set his lamp down. By its flickering light he studied his map and the room. "Atok the Million-Eyed..." He smiled mischievously then put the map away and strode confidently to the well. "Shelvox, what strange paths you have wandered, my cadre."

Ka removed his goggles and took up his lamp; strange shadows flitted across the stones like dancing gremlins. Going to the west wall, his hands found a secret doorway in the stone, nearly concealed by the branching roots; he blew white dust from the crack between the door and the jamb. He pressed it firmly, shoved it with his shoulder, and it opened incrementally; the roots snapped and popped as it did. Ka's light revealed a long, tapering corridor.

Pardew looked on; his wrinkled brow demonstrated how impressed he was. "Thanks be to your map," he said. Ka smiled.

They entered, pressed the door closed behind them, and began walking, their footfalls dully pattering on stone. After several paces, they reached an archway leading into a new chamber at the end of the corridor.

"Let me go before you," Pardew said, sword in hand. When they came into the chamber, they saw that at the center was a large, shadowy grotto. Over the grotto hung a strange formation of stone, a hook or pulley, and this was shaped by a sculptor to resemble a squatting, fat-bellied demon whose forking tongue lolled from its grinning mouth. Pardew hesitantly approached the blackness. He peered into the hole and could see mostly darkness and a few vague shapes at the bottom, the suggestion of several jawless skulls.

Pardew withdrew from the hole with a shiver.

"An oubliette," said Ka. "Shelvox had many enemies. Let us move on." He motioned to the corridor that continued beyond this chamber.

Pardew and Ka continued as crabs scuttling from one hole to another. When they issued into the room, they were immediately disoriented by a strange phenomenon. Ka's lantern light seemed to multiply; several orbs of lamplight swung in the chamber. Great polished panels lined the walls and even plated the domed and arched ceiling. Although some panels were begrimed with dirt, Pardew was surprised by the crystal clarity of most of them. Several Pardews and Kas held hooded lamps, stroked beards, and hoisted article-laden belt pouches.

"By Ral's Grove, this is beautiful," Pardew whispered.

Pardew approached a wall and using the sleeve of his cloak, he wiped away a spot of dust, revealed a small patch of reflective surface. He locked eyes with himself.

His eyes were bloodshot, his cheeks gaunt and hungry. His face was covered in soot from the greasy smoke from the torch fires above. His beard had pieces of ash stuck in it.

"Mirrors," he said grinning.

"No simple mirrors, these," whispered Ka, placing his hand on the wall, palm to palm with one of his reflections. "These are doorways to worlds unknown. We would be wise to move on."

When they came to the next room, they saw that in the center of this chamber was a raised stone dais on a stage. There were several bizarre formations of what might be furniture strewn throughout the room crumbling to dust; the non-human bodies they might have served would have been strange indeed. There was also an archway opening out into a hallway, flanked by moldy banners.

For a moment, Pardew and Ka just stood there, anchored in indecision.

Pardew removed the Jorum from his pack, held it out for Ka to take. "As good a spot as any for your study of the Jorum," said Pardew. "Can you make it sing?"

But before he transferred it to Ka, three trumpets of a horn sounded sharply; red light and twisting shadows bloomed beyond the archway.

The devil rabble pursued.

Pardew clumsily dropped the Jorum, and it nearly fell to the ground; Ka lurched and juggled it into his arms.

Several of the red devils issued into the room from the archway wielding short knives and spears. The companions turned their gaze, and likewise, from the other room, the Chamber of Mirrors, a smaller company of devils charged in in a clumsy formation, their blades flashing, their pupils trembling pinpoints of rage.

There was no escape. They were trapped and must fight.

Pardew unsheathed his two blades, his own and his dead brother's, and shouted, "Bellik!" With these blades gripped tightly, he lunged past Ka at the devils issuing from the Chamber of Mirrors, and so became a bearded, howling, frothing man-giant. Ka, meanwhile, held the Jorum aloft and began shouting incantation after incantation.

Pardew was no martial artist trained for battlefield fighting but a brawler whose swordplay had been honed in the fighting pits. He did not fight with the technician's skill but with the artist's intuition: he ranged his sword clumsily, swiped and stabbed, hewed spearheads, hove shields, and hissed as his blade was turned, parried, and dodged by swift feet. So, when he drew black blood, he surprised himself as much as his foe, who writhed and tugged at his dead brother's blade lodged deeply in the stringy muscles of its neck. Pardew left it there.

The battle was a nightmarish confusion of screaming arrows, sharp teeth, hot sprays of blood, and hissing, falsetto voices cursing and chanting, and yet somehow they battled through the smaller company of devils and came to the Chamber of Mirrors, Pardew holding a bleeding wound and Ka screaming at the Jorum twinkling in his cupped hands.

Fleeing with his own dripping blade, Pardew was made queasy by his kaleidoscopic reflections twisting and convulsing over several walls; his head spun, his wet blade clattered to the floor, and he stumbled past Ka through the door of the oubliette chamber.

It was because of this disorientation that when he entered there he forgot the grotto pit; his ankle rolled on the edge and shrieking he fell, headlong and over, into the darkness.

But then he hit, smashed into a pile of debris that stuffed the oubliette full. His breath fled as smoke before a gust of wind. Great waves of pain pulsed through his body. Grunting, hissing, he tried to rise, but the debris shifted beneath him. And just as he did so the creatures rushed into the room, trumpeting black horns, screaming, their many feet pattering on the floor.

They circled the oubliette. Their pointy-eared heads stared down at him. They stood in clumsy ranks, haughty, leaning on their spears, fingering their black, curving blades crudely wrought, grinning cruelly, snarling, displaying scornful sharp teeth set in wide grimaces. Their red torches threw light into the hole, and Pardew saw he was waist deep in bones: skulls, ribs, hips, femurs, jaws, some bones human, others vaguely human in cast.

The demonfolk laughed above. They knew they had him trapped and were in no hurry to put an end to such a rare entertainment.

"Holy man! Holy man! Trapped like a rabbit in a bone pit!" said one of them in a high-pitched, nasal voice.

"Let's cover him in red coals and cook him slow!" shouted another, its voice like an excited child.

Hearing their dark singing, Pardew didn't know what to do, couldn't imagine any manner of egress. His eyes darted left and right. "Ka!" he shouted. "Make the Jorum sing!" At any moment they would end him, he thought. They would spit him with their many spears and carry him to their coal pit, smoke him, and after he had cooked thoroughly, they would pull his greasy flesh from his bones.

He closed his eyes and began whispering to his brother's shade: "Bellik. My brother, I seem to have failed you. Perhaps this trial was too great." He pitied himself profoundly, thought back to the long journey that had brought him to this red end.

A screaming arrow was loosed, its head buried deep in Pardew's left breast. Pardew howled in pain and writhed in the pit. He screamed and frothed with pain as he pulled the blood-streaked missile from his wound, saliva dripping from his lips. Pain vibrated there, and soaking blood bloomed on the fabric of his soiled habit.

Darkness pressed the periphery of his vision; he felt dizzy and knew unconsciousness would take him soon, and then a deeper darkness. A million succeeding memories flitted across his mind, ephemeral and fragmentary as words caught randomly on a book's pages swiftly turned: "I failed you, brother," he whispered to himself.

Just then, coming from not far off, a note rang high and clear and long and flowed like liquid mercury over curving glass; it spread, dancing ripples of sacred sound, expressing a beautiful truth without words. The note increased in intensity until waves of it undulated through the cavern and seemed to bend the very fabric of reality. From Pardew's perspective, the granlings, the pit, the flames of their torches, all wavered as if seen through water.

Granlings stood, transfixed, rooted firmly, their tongues cleaving to their palates, and the expressions of their faces changed from anger, to surprise, and then—to utter passivity.

Eventually the ringing note diminished and was gone. Pardew glanced up at the granlings who encircled the oubliette opening above. To his surprise, the haughty granlings were speechless. They gazed into nothingness, their eyes glassy and distant, holding their weapons but loosely as well as their torches that flickered and dripped fuel in sizzling drops.

Pardew hoped.

"Ka!" he shouted, his voice, though pained, was falsetto in euphoria. There was no answer. "Ka! Have you done it?"

Pardew could barely believe this; his stomach tightened and his hands trembled in exultation.

Tears pooled in his eyes and he gritted his teeth as the pain of his wound pulsed deeper; he placed a hand on the wound and felt wetness, and when he removed it, it was stained red.

He looked up.

"Ka, I'm bleeding!" Still there was no answer. Pardew licked his lips. "Lower me a looped rope! I have strength yet!"

Then he heard the sound of sandals on stone. At the vertex of the oubliette stood Ka leaning over and in. The sorcerer looked down on him with reptile eyes, and he held the Jorum in one hand.

"Are you hurt?" he shouted down.

The black pupils of the granlings, hitherto shrunk to pinpoints, widened into black orbs.

"Yes, but not from the fall," Pardew replied. "They skewered me with one of their arrows."

"Unfortunate," said Ka. "One moment." He disappeared for the few beats and returned, unlacing a parcel; he removed something fist-sized and white. "Take this!" said Ka, tossing the object. Pardew caught it. It was a sticky, cloth-like substance. "A medicinal poultice, a mixture of a certain spider's web, lizard's ichor, and the ink of the doom of Inmor'leh. Apply it your wound. Not only will it staunch the flow of blood but it will heal the laceration, leaving only a pale scar."

Ka applied the poultice and hissed as the wound hissed and bubbled and burned. He could not restrain himself; a hoarse groan escaped his lips. "The pain is unfortunate but nevertheless an indication of the poultice's efficacy," said Ka. "Is your wound healed?" The granlings still swayed, unmoving, clustering around Ka like living statues.

Pardew probed his wound with fingers; wiping away slime and blood, he was surprised to find it healed, its only record, a slightly textured scar.

"It is! My thanks!" Pardew said. "Now, bring a looped rope, my friend! There is an appropriate cord in my pack, which I dropped as I fled!"

Ka glanced over his shoulder and yet stood unmoving. He licked his lips.

"Pardew," he shouted, almost consolingly. He licked his lips. "I have a confession, a sin, if you will, I would like to air." Pardew's heart lurched in his chest. "On our first night together, as you slept, your robes fell open at your neck, and I noted a latched amulet there, a black triangle. I thought little of it, thinking it but a symbol of your faith, but the shape of it gnawed on me. You see, your brother speaks of a triangle of iron and three symbols, three ideograms, that, if known, would unlock the mystery of the Hearthfather's name."

Sweat bloomed on Pardew's forehead. He gritted his teeth.

"The correlation was too suggestive, and so I sought to open your amulet, expecting a secret. But I was unable to, for you woke even as I outstretched my hand. That is my confession."

Pardew tried to speak, to say something, but his voice was a hoarse croaking.

"My friend," said Ka. "My curiosity is unbearable: what do you keep in that latched amulet?"

Pardew frowned. "You know it is a secret!" he shouted.

Ka nodded solemnly and stroked his triangular beard. When he stood, the torchlight shadowed his face, the dark hollows of his eyes and cheeks, and from Pardew's perspective, he seemed less a man than a tall darkness embodied: "Of course it is a secret, but hunger, thirst, and time: they are fierce foes. I would never harm you, my friend. I have learned affection and have some store of it. But, friendship is a flimsy wraith, and I would have the secret of your black triangle. So, think on that for a while and learn wisdom!" At this he turned and left, the granlings following him and simpering almost as if they were his supplicants.

Animalized by rage, Pardew howled and cursed at the empty air, a dark song in a dark place.

Jason Carney has published stories in Skelos, Hypnos Magazine, Swords and Sorcery Magazine, Swords Against Cthulhu II, Empyreome, Heroic Fantasy Quarterly and others.

Amsel the Immortal

By LAUREN GOFF

For some, immortality might seem a blessing, but for Amsel, it is a curse! The sorcerer who discovered the key to perpetual regeneration finds himself the tortured prisoner and test subject of the Royal College...until a woman releases him!

The day I started on my journey was the day I met Nita. I was in my room in the Althean Chancellor's Royal College, specifically the biology laboratory, as I had been for the past ten years. My room was small and confined, and contained only a stool, a pile of hay, and a bucket. Well, those items, and a table that I was to be bolted onto when the need arose. The scientists who kept me there were kind enough to give me a window, but it was high and stick-thin—I could not see the outside world, and it let through only a little light at noon. I was lying on my back on the operating table, bolted through the ribs to the cool wood by which I was soothing the burning sensation that accompanied the scientists taking fresh samples of tissues from my back. It would heal back within ten minutes or so, but the regeneration process could not take away the septic, creeping heat that my skin had left behind.

I heard someone moving things around in the surgical area outside the cell door. Whoever it was shuffled papers, pulled open drawers, lifted knives from their places on the table, and finally settled down at a table to scratch out page after page of something with a quill, all the while being as quiet as humanly possible. If I were not as attuned to the noises of the place and the infrequent human interaction, I imagine I would not have noticed. At the time, I assumed it was the freckled assistant that had recently joined the other scientists. Note-taking was a task usually delegated to underlings. I was a bit surprised, however, because they had all left that morning for a College banquet put on by the Chancellor to celebrate the institution's one hundred and seventy-fifth anniversary. That was why they had kept me bolted to the operating table after they left: they did not want me to escape in their absence. Despite this, I had looked forward to a day free of observation by those talentless hacks, but it seemed my awful luck had robbed me of even that.

The person outside wrote like that for what I thought was several hours, though it was hard to tell. The burn of the missing skin soon melted away as it regrew. That allowed me to appreciate the familiar pain of the bolts in my hips, shoulders, and knees. I dully counted the circles on my chest that a fly made, unable to entertain much more advanced thought through the sticky pain.

Soon, I supposed, the freckled apprentice would come back in here to gather more samples, or perhaps give me some table scraps from the banquet that he came from. Or he could beat me, which was more likely given his new master's disposition. The fly made seven circles before it left and rubbed its little hands together on mine. I noticed that the moss growing up near the high ceiling across from the window had grown some tiny white flowers, almost imperceptible from down below.

My silent companion got up and walked down the hallway. I heard her jiggling the handle of a locked door, scraping a bit at them with what sounded like metal sticks, and opening the door and walking further away. It struck me then that it was not a scientist. The realization was so outlandish to me that I felt numb for a minute or so, unable to stop the sound of lockpicks from repeating in my head. An outsider. In here. Not a scientist. I called out almost as a reflex.

"Thief! Help me! I'm in here!" The faint noises in the other room stopped suddenly, but no one came. "Come on! I'm trapped in here, and I want to leave! I hate these scientists as much as you!" My voice cracked at the end from lack of use. The intruder crept forward slowly and entered the hallway, stopping at the end. She tried the door across from me and started to try and open the one beside me.

"No, to your right! There's a false wall. Pull the sconce at the end." The intruder stopped in front of my door, but did not do as I asked.

"Who are you?" she asked, her voice muffled through the door. It was hard to gauge her emotion through the thick door, but she sounded nervous.

"My name is Lord Oskar Amsel. I have been imprisoned here for ten years because I refused to give up my research to the old Chancellor at his *whim*." I could not put as much invective into this statement as I wanted to, but enough seems to have been communicated for the intruder to open the door as I asked.

The woman I saw before me was dressed in what I imagined to be what regular women wore then: a simple red dress with puffed sleeves, boots, and a white headscarf. She carried an overstuffed bag filled mostly with papers, a thick canvas sash, and a *bauern-wehr*, which she had drawn. What was strangest about her was that she clearly wasn't Althean. She did have straight black hair, it is true, but her skin was oak brown, her cheekbones were wider and higher, and her nose more prominent. There were not very many foreigners in the Althean capital when I was free, only in the subjugated territories. It seemed she was as surprised by my appearance as I was of her, because she let out a little gasp. It would make sense, I suppose. I was a man bolted to a table with an attached blood drainage system, with a matted beard and hair that went to his hips. The room's smell was fetid.

"I believe you need to introduce yourself," I said.

"You can call me Nita. Gods. What...what happened? Why are you here?" Just then, there was a sound in the far room. The head scientist and her right-hand man were talking loudly. They sounded drunk, and they opened a door downstairs with a clatter. Nita looked at me with panic and ran over, attempting to pull out the bolts with her hands.

"Just cut off my head!" I whispered with as much authority as I could muster. "There's not enough time!" She looked at me in disgust. "Trust me! I'll survive! Do it!"

She took a look at her bag filled with notes, closed her eyes, and took a deep breath. She worked fast once she set her mind on the task: it only took three swings of her knife. Once my head was free, the lattices of pain that seemed embedded in my body drifted away like cobwebs, leaving only the pain in my neck. Nita lifted me up and looked at me, almost fully expecting me to be dead. I could not talk because my lungs and diaphragm were on the table, but I smiled as wide as I could at her. Her face went pale and it looked like she would drop me, but instead she put me inside the canvas sash she wore around her shoulders and left.

It had been eight years since I had seen outside of my cell. It sounds silly, but there was so much to focus on, and so much depth in the rooms outside of my small room, that I felt blinded. There was the beautifully-carpeted hallway of storage space and offices that led to my cell. I could make out the whorls of carved sycamore leaves as Nita sped to the main laboratory and operating theater. There, on the metal table in the center of the creamy yellow room, were what I assumed to be my tissue samples, on trays of ice and floating suspended in various mixtures. There was a cadaver on the table next to them, along with other tissue samples and associated implements. As horrific as this place had been to me, I felt a pure, weightless feeling.

Nita turned and headed towards a side exit to a balcony that was on the left side of the room, next to a set of windows facing the brick building next door. Her hand just reached the exit's old ring handle when the head scientist and her fat lackey stumbled into the room from the stairwell. They saw Nita, and they saw my head in the canvas sash, staring at them. For a sickening moment, they paused, mouths opened stupidly, like kine chewing their cud, but they soon rushed in. Nita instinctively turned to look, but turned back and wrenched the door open. She climbed over the balcony's chalky-white bannister, grabbed onto a rope that she had apparently tied to it, and lowered herself down so fast that the rope below us started wriggling.

Our pursuers' heads came into view over the bannister, and they started trying to untie the rope, which sent tremors down its fibers. Nita hissed what I assume to be curses in her language and started descending faster. The head scientist disappeared from sight and reappeared with a still-bloody bonesaw. She lost no time in applying it to the rope. At that point, we were almost to the first story. Nita saw the bonesaw and swung to her right so that she almost touched the biology building. We heard a fibrous ripping sound and shot down an inch. Nita swung forward again and touched the building, scrabbling over the rough bricks and gripping a couple that stuck out. Then, the rope dropped behind us, descending in heavy spirals. Nita was able to scramble down the remaining story, though her fingers bled. She folded me up in the canvas sash so I could no longer see my environment beyond it, and she ran for several terrifying minutes, through quiet and busy streets. Eventually, when she opened the door to a smoky-smelling building, I knew I was safe for a time.

Nita kept me in a dusty storage room that smelled faintly of rust for a few hours, but then moved me to a root cellar somewhere else. From the sounds I could hear from outside the house, it was on the outskirts of town. Nita did not visit the house, but a female gardener of some sort, presumably a friend, checked on me only once or twice in the two days it took for the rest of my body to regrow, darting her head through the door at the top of the dirt stairs. I do not blame her—the process is disquieting. I myself could not stand to look at it the first time I had my head cut off in the riots following the grain shortages fifty years ago. The young man who did it, a skinny, frightened baker's boy, took my head and threw it in a stinking pile of other well-dressed bodies. Now, after escaping the pain of being bolted to the table, it was oddly comforting. The thought that I would have a new body that they had not touched kept reoccurring. After the process was over, the gardener poked her head in, as per usual, and gasped when she found me sitting up on the floor.

"Ah, excellent. Bring me some clothes at once, goodwife, along with a razor, a basin of water, a mirror, and soap," I said. She nodded mutely, stumbled back, and did as I asked. I was shaving my beard when Nita returned, this time covered in soot and wearing a blacksmith's clothes. I saw both her and her friend walk down the stairs in the mirror I had been provided.

"Nita. I am pleased to see you have not yet been arrested. I almost failed to recognize you," I said as I cut off the beard below my chin.

"Yeah, I'm happy, too. Lord Amsel, this is Enid," she said, gesturing to the gardener. "You can count on her not telling any Chancellor's men about you, but it won't be long before they figure out I'm the document thief and then follow my movements to here and my master's smithy. I'm going to deposit what I stole at a dead drop outside of the city limits, and then you're going to help me get out of the Empire." Her sharpness made me frown as I glided the knife over my skin, relishing the feeling of the dead weight of matted, soapy hair drop from my face. I sighed, partly in relief, and partly from displeasure.

"If I am going to take any orders from you, you will explain to me what you were doing with the information in the first place. I follow people rarely, and people I know nothing about never."

"What does it—fine. You've noticed I am not Althean, correct?"

I nodded, and then began grouping my

wet hair at the point I would soon cut it.

"Well, I'm from an island in the west that the Empire is getting awfully close to. My chief decided we needed to find out how to make these metal weapons you're using ourselves. So, he sent me to where the best blacksmiths are because I had learned your language from traders."

"That explains the getup, but not why you were poking around the College, where, if you remember, they study biology and other such things. Not that I am complaining, of course."

She growled in frustration, running a hand through her hair.

"Does it matter? I rescued you, and now I'm *ruined*."

"Oh, excuse me. I apologize. But you cannot *know* that the Chancellor's men will find you. You look extremely different than before, as I said. Why drag me along?"

She pushed past her friend and marched right behind me as I started to rinse the soap out of my hair, which was then only shoulder-length. When I sat up and turned to see her looming behind me, I almost fell over as I scrambled away in pure, electrifying fear instinct. She laughed coldly.

"Look, your excellency. It won't take much time to narrow the list of tribal women down to say, ten or fifteen. Then, they start whittling the list down, questioning each one carefully, more likely than not cruelly. Then, sooner or later, they get to *me*." She strode closer to me, closing the distance I had crawled.

"'Just go home,' you might say, like a fool. I'll tell you why not. Because then that's all the excuse anyone needs to begin *really* conquering us. At least if I'm never found, they won't have a clear reason." She seemed to lose stream when I raised up my arms to shield my face, breathing raggedly. Behind my closed eyes, I was seeing visions of the head scientist towering over me.

"I...I'm sorry. It's not your fault. It's not your fault," she said, drawing a hand across her eyes. "I just figure you need to leave the city, too, since they know exactly what you look like, and your...condition is probably valuable to their research. So, please. Leave with me in the morning?" I could not answer, but I managed to nod.

"And so, that's why they haven't been able to get any results for the royal family! I keep telling them the wrong recipes, but even if I didn't they probably wouldn't work without the right timing and the right placement. I know it sounds like magic, but really, these forces are as natural as, oh, dirt or trees! The same thing controls whether or not making a golem is successful, if you know anything about that," I said, unable to contain my excitement at having someone to talk to. We had just left a small fishing village by the Blackvein, the main river that flowed through the capital. It was about twenty miles east of the outskirts, and we had been riding for almost a full day.

The rolling hills surrounding the fishing village gave way to a plain filled with upright stones. They were just as moss-covered as I left them years ago. The fields of grass, glistening in the sun like emeralds, looked much the same as well. I suppose it stood to reason, but the fact surprised me nonetheless, as the fabric of the world seemed to have changed every other way in my absence. The capital was bigger, to be sure: the buildings were taller and thinner, and it was getting so crowded in some places that people were starting to live underground. There were more foreigners about, and more exotic goods were being sold: strange, spiky fruit, spices, fine fabrics. The areas where the Eastermen were allowed to hawk their wares were the most interesting. The Eastern kingdoms were not on as cordial terms when I had been free previously, so the delicate paintings they sold captivated me more than they probably should have.

We were nearing a fork in the road with the waystone where the dead drop was. Nita nodded to me and trotted her bay horse over to a beech tree behind the stone. She was able to climb up to a fork in the branches like it was nothing and soon placed the treated wooden cylinder containing her notes and tools in its dark boughs. She looked up at the tree after she clambered down, its leaves creating dappled light on her face. It almost looked like she was underwater.

"So. Let's go to the Eastern Kingdoms," she said, finally.

"Indeed. I am glad we have chosen that as our destination, you know. I imagine I will be able to find research I have never come across before. Imagine! Libraries of things never seen by an Althean!" I said, waving my hand in an arc for emphasis. That got Nita to smile.

"…of course, that is assuming I have not cured myself on the way there," I stated.

"Hmm! I can learn all sorts of languages there, and—huh? 'Cured yourself?'" she said, slowing her horse down.

"Yes. You cannot imagine I would want to live forever, could you?" I had not slowed down my horse, so she started to fall behind.

"I did, honestly," she said, bringing herself up to speed again. "Why wouldn't you?"

"Heh. That is none of your concern, dearie. I have a plan that should work better than playing my wrists like a violin, and it just so happens it involves a volcano that is on your way to your libraries. It should not take long." She nodded, still looking at me like I was some alien creature.

Nita and I kept in the shadow of the pine trees in our approach to the volcano. Live trees, their trunks almost as white as ivory, were fused to the blasted husks of ones that had been alive when the mountain last erupted. It was easy for me to imagine what it looked like back then: clouds of sulfurous ash clinging to the ground that the lava had peeled of life, trees burning, landscape rendered unrecognizable by rivers of the earth's hot blood. Even after hundreds of years, the rolling hills I saw behind us in the sunset are covered in black rock and tree skeletons. A fitting place to make an attempt to die.

"You know, your excellency, this mountain isn't active. Doesn't have lava in it," said Nita. I noticed she had caught up to me and was looking up at me with that amused and confused expression she employed so often.

"I'm not planning on jumping in. Even if there were lava, I would just sit on the top of it, burning and regenerating for all eternity. Or until you feel like fishing me out, which would be quite dangerous," I said. It came out harsher than I intended, but it did not seem that she was bothered.

"All right. Tell me you don't need to climb all the way into the crater to access these energies you want to harness. The border guards might come by the other side of the mountain early." She had taken out the map the smuggler from the last town had drawn on.

"No, the ancient savages used a cave near the base of the mountain to make their sacrifices. Hopefully repeating the ritual there, in a place of such aberrant natural energies, will do the trick. It will be quick, whatever the outcome. All *you* have to do is use my dagger to stab me in the heart. You probably do not know this, but bronze amplifies the potency of energy loci, like the one atop of this cinder cone. The ancient savages who used the mountain to…" She sighed and sat down in the shadow of one of the many gorse bushes that clung to the blasted landscape and motioned me to sit down beside her.

"…to make their sacrifices to their gods probably knew this, so they used bronze daggers to kill people, too. You know, I am not used to people ignoring me."

"I already knew the bit about the bronze, sir, but thank you for thinking of my intellectual needs. Come here," Nita snapped. I walked over to look at the map. In the middle of the map, which Nita seemed to have torn from an atlas in her master's workshop, the figure of the volcano waited. It was bisected by a line that said "Eastern Kingdoms" on one side and "Altheus Empire" on the other. She tapped a hairline fissure on our side, the Althean side, which apparently corresponded to the crack in the ground next to our copse of trees that was big enough to sail a ferry down. That is, had there been any water in it.

"This route leads past a cave on the Eastern side, as well as a good series of boulders to lose patrols in. Or so Agathe told me. Now, this might be the cave you were talking about the 'savages' using, if we have any luck left. We can take it to the cave, where I'll kill you. Then I'll go here to sleep." She tapped an X drawn just past a pond. "It's a safe house that the smugglers use. You can meet me there if it doesn't quite work out and you can't move for a bit. There's a hatch under some loose ash and lichen. Near where there are some flat rocks that lie on each other like a triangle." I nodded, but felt apprehension. Nita got up and turned towards the mountain.

The entrance to the cave had two stone sculptures on either side. One was of a snake coiled up, its scales carved like tongues of fire. The other was of a weeping person covering their face with their hands. Inside, it was quite dark, but at least it was dry. There was a stone slab with carvings of birds on its surface in the middle of a ring of dusty purple geodes. I felt my throat tighten, and I reflexively ran my hand through my hair several times before handing my rondel to Nita, who polished it on her faded gambeson.

"R-right. I will just...get on the slab then." She looked at me but said nothing. Even on the slab, the only thing I could feel was a bit of the cold wind coming from the desert to the west as it rapidly cooled. I had hoped it would feel powerful, somehow, but apparently, these Places of Power were as disappointing as the immortality I had slaved for in my youth, one hundred and forty-six years ago. I unlaced my shirt so that my clavicles were exposed—an easy route for the rondel to take. I smoothed the poor jacket I'd managed to grab before we left the city, made sure my hair was in order once more, and crossed my hands over my stomach, as I had seen undertakers do with corpses before they sealed them in the wall of the city. Nita walked over and touched the cold tip of the knife to my chest, bracing herself by holding my shoulder near my neck.

"Nita. I think it will work this time, don't you?" I said, in an unexpectedly shaky voice. I had meant to sound encouraging. Years and years not talking to anyone will make it hard to speak properly, I told myself. I believed that excuse, too, until the pinprick pain of tears emerged in the corners of my eyes. Nita, for her part, pursed her lips in a sad smile, and murmured something in the language of the coastal savages.

"If I've ever wronged you in any way, please forgive me," I said. "Thank you for taking me out of that attic." She nodded, not breaking my gaze.

"Before we do this, I've got to ask you again. I know the College was horrific, but is your life so bad right now? Don't you want to enjoy life as much as possible?" Images of the people and animals I'd chained in my laboratory returned to me after she asked that question. In my mind, I fed them draught after draught, brewed with the inspiration that came to me after sleepless nights with books bound in human skin. I hurt them, again and again. They died each time, faces pale with fear, until my manservant Joachim was the only one left. When his head was still looking around, mouth moving, for an hour after I had severed it, I was so filled with ecstasy that I threw it in the air before reattaching it to his neck. "We're perfect! We're perfect now!" I think I said, though I can't be sure. Memory is such a flimsy thing.

Nita had closed her eyes and was continuing to murmur. The cold of the knife still at the top of my chest was making my heart thump painfully.

"I did it to prove a point. Now that that hypothesis has been disproven, I don't feel the need to be here anymore. The means to this life was an abomination, so keeping it seems...wrong." Nita huffed, and removed my rondel from my skin, biting her lip.

"I suppose you're right. I...yeah," she rambled, seeming to talk to herself more so than me. I suppose she, too, thought this attempt would be more successful.

"Just do it! Please!"

"Go in freedom, Amsel," Nita said.

She took a deep breath and put the knife back to where it was. This time her hand gripped my shoulder tighter. She plunged my rondel down behind my ribs and into my heart. I felt something warm burst in my chest, and I screamed. The knife was a shard of ice, and the networks of my blood vessels were filled with burning oil. Then, I felt like someone else was there, watching us, but when I grabbed Nita's hands to warn her, she was already gone. I heard voices in the distance, and my vision turned white.

I was back in my old garden, sitting under the gazebo Father built. The sun was shining, birds were chirping, and Joachim was there, pruning the rosebushes. A giant snake, its entire body consumed by purple flames, inched its way across the lawn, leaving a line of wildflowers in its wake. The oak hydrangeas near my chair rustled in the breeze, and I took a drink from my glass of wine. I heard a voice from beside me that made my hand go limp. I let my glass slip to the floor and it shattered into ashes and the shards of purple geodes. The timbers of the gazebo shuddered, and when I looked back at the garden all of the plants had their roots in the air instead of their leaves and flowers. I could not understand what the voice said.

The first thing I heard when I awoke was the familiar sound of the wind slithering through the rocks. It was warm, but because there was so little pink light coming through the rough blanket covering my face that I had trouble discerning that I was no longer unconscious. My chest still ached, but it did not burn. When I threw off the blanket and stuck my finger in the dagger wound, I could not push it through all the way. I knew from experience that I shouldn't try to sit up after suffering a severe chest wound, so I rolled over and shielded my face from the sun. I was at a deserted campsite within the mostly-collapsed walls of a dried lava bubble. I judged from the position of the sun that it was about six hours until noon. There were a few used bowls of what looked like extraordinarily pale rice and a hatchet sitting around the still-smoldering campfire. I grabbed the hatchet, just in case.

I rolled onto my knees and moved my neck slowly from side to side, feeling my fingers and toes prickle. Then, I stood up and looked around. The camp seemed to be on a small ridge farther to the east of the volcano than the cave. There were criss-crossing networks of ditches, river beds, and boulders surrounding me, and to my right I could see a good-sized pond half a mile away. Farther to my right, a patch of trees made an arc that was mostly free of the criss-crossings of the rock maze and made it twenty feet away from the banks of the pond.

There were no patrol officers on the way to the pond, but I saw a group of them on the far side. There was a ring around the triangle rocks that Nita had described, and others were combing through the surrounding area, presumably looking for another entrance. They had rolled several heavy

Out Of The Ruins

A NOVEL BY
LEN GILBERT

rocks beside where I assume the entrance was, and one of them was shouting in our language down at it. "In one minute….come out….close….starve…"

I could see Nita emerge from the ground and be tied up by her wrists and ankles shortly thereafter. They regrouped and started marching her back towards my position and their camp. I followed them back to the site, through the trees. The one who could speak our language, a tall man, seemed to interrogate her on the way, though I could not hear their conversation.

They were nearing the camp then, and I would not be able to interfere as easily in their stone enclosure. I did not have time for an elegant plan. I charged down the hill with the hatchet out, shirt still bloody from the stabbing, yelling as loudly as I could

when I got close to the band. The first one I went for was the translator officer. I slashed at his arms swiftly, so I could bring the hatchet around to the other officers as quickly as possible. I laid a deep gash on his arm, and he cradled it close to his chest, falling backwards and backing away. The other officers seemed too afraid to use their strength in numbers to advance on me, and indeed a couple ran off, screaming. I suppose they thought I had been dead when they found me.

I swung the hatchet around my head, threatening officers who remained, and then bent down to cut the ropes on Nita's legs. There was a small length of rope trailing from either of her ankles, but she was still able to sprint past the three officers that formed the back of the party. A few canny ones tried to start off after her, but I was able to catch them in the back before I got taken down and restrained. I watched Nita run off into the distance, past the grove of trees and over a hill of grassy shrubs as they bound me. I do not know if she will get to where she needs to go, but I have high confidence in her.

Lauren Goff is a Native Speaker and writer working in Iwate, Japan. She has enjoyed fantasy and horror since a young age, and has recently discovered a liking for creative nonfiction. Major influences on her writing include JRR Tolkien (surprising no one), Kelly Link, Agatha Christie, and Anthony Bloom. Her current ambition is to train her students to fight her enemies and gain control of the capitol through guerilla warfare. Eventually becoming an editor of a small magazine and going to graduate school would also be nice, though. She blogs at https://www.eighthdayblog.com/. Please address all serious or nonserious questions to lauren.goff@yahoo.com

An Interrupted Scandal

By MISHA BURNETT

The Free City of Dracoheim is a city of mystery and crime—and where there is crime, there must be investigation and there must be justice! To solve the most beastly of the city's crimes, the brilliant Dr. Linus Fell must himself become a beast!

When a crime is reported within the borders of the Free City of Dracoheim, the initial call is taken by the local constabulary office. Each area of the City—District, Township, Parish, or Principality—has its own constables. If the responsible officer of the watch judges the crime to be a minor affair, it will be investigated on the constabulary level, and the criminal, if found, will stand before the local magistrate for sentencing.

Serious crimes are escalated to the City Police, which is organized in Bureaus; Violence & Murder, Major Theft, Fraud, Unlicensed Magic, Vice and Special Investigations. In addition, there is the Committee For Public Safety, which is concerned with crimes that directly affect the office of the Lord Mayor, and the Department of External Affairs, which handles crimes committed by or against resident aliens within the City.

Furthermore, many City offices—for example the Department of Indigenous Affairs, the Waterways Authority, the Commercial & Industrial Regulations Board, and the Office of External Trade—maintain their own staff of investigators who are empowered to bring criminal cases to the City Courts.

Despite this rather bewildering system of interlocking jurisdictions, the wheels of justice in Dracoheim, when properly lubricated, grind with surprising speed and efficiency.

The murder of Cornelius Mordred can serve as an example.

The Watch Officer of the Breckinridge Park Constabulary had scarcely finished logging the call when he picked up his direct line to the City Police and escalated the matter, relating the particulars of the crime with evident relief that case was no longer on his desk.

The Captain of Detectives of the Violence & Murder Bureau would have ordinarily handled the matter; however, he elected to transfer the case to Special Investigations, citing the celebrity of the victim and the need for discretion as an excuse.

The Captain of Detectives of Special Investigations in turn placed a call—dialing the number himself rather than placing it through the police switchboard—to one of his senior investigators, a man called Vetch. The Captain gave Vetch very specific instructions regarding the case.

Once Inspector Vetch, who had been enjoying a cup of coffee and a poached egg in his modest townhouse, hung up the phone, he gave a sharp glance to his wife. Knowing his moods, she took her own breakfast out to the balcony to give him privacy.

The Inspector then made one more call, to an old friend who was in no official way associated with any of the City's array of law enforcement agencies.

It wasn't much more than an hour after the initial call that Inspector Vetch drove his departmental car to the tradesman entrance of the Pembroke Arms. Police—even a senior investigator for City Special Investigations—used the back doors in Breckinridge Park. The park which gave the township its name contained a hothouse garden stocked with flowers imported from Verdemaire—complete with incubi guest workers to tend them. The meanest apartment in the Pembroke Arms would command a rent equal to twice the local Watch Officer's wages.

"This is going to be ugly," Vetch muttered to his companion as they left his unmarked car.

"Tell me nothing of the case," the other said softly. "I must observe the facts *tabula rasa*."

Vetch frowned. "The papers, I meant," he said defensively. "They'll have front page fodder for weeks. That's just the nature of the principals, nothing to do with the crime."

"The nature of the principals defines the nature of the crime," the other replied.

Vetch was silent. Inwardly he reviewed the call he'd received that morning.

We need this wrapped up fast, the Chief of Detectives had said. *I'm already getting pressure from Parliament, and it's going to get worse once the press gets involved. I need this solved, and I need it solved now—there can't be any doubt. Call your mad friend, and give him a free hand. I want a murderer in custody before the afternoon papers hit the streets. Is that clear?*

Crystal clear, boss, Vetch thought. But he kept his thoughts to himself.

Silence suited him. He was a big man with the physique of a wrestler and the face of a battle-scarred longshoreman. He gave the impression of being extraordinarily strong and immensely stupid. Only the first of those was true. Inspector Vetch's given name was Rodger. There were rumors that his wife used it upon occasion, but that had never been proven.

The man who accompanied Inspector Vetch down the alley to the rear entrance was not an imposing figure. He was a bit shorter than average, considerably thinner than most, and his suit was serviceable only, being of an uninspired cut and several years old. Nonetheless, the pair of uniformed constables stationed at the door stiffened upon catching sight of him. One pulled open the door while the other saluted the Inspector.

After the Inspector and his guest had passed, and the door firmly closed behind them, the two constables shared a look.

"Dr. Fell," one whispered to the other. "They've brought in Dr. Fell!"

Linus Fell, for it was that celebrated physician and criminologist, seemed embarrassed by the attention. Inspector Vetch, as was his custom, seemed to take no notice of anything, giving the appearance of a sleepwalker, but in fact he missed nothing.

Together the two men entered the lobby of the high-rise. At the concierge desk stood a well-dressed plainclothes detective from the Murder Squad.

"Let me see the log, Tucker," Vetch said, "We're going on up."

Tucker handed a clipboard to Vetch, who scanned it and then wrote "Dr. L. Fell" and "Insp. Vetch" and "07:19" and "consultation" in the relevant blanks.

"Three men upstairs?" Vetch asked.

Tucker nodded. "Two coroner's deputies and Sergeant Galgol of the Witchfinders. He's a good man."

"That's all you have securing the scene?" Vetch frowned.

"The only way out of the penthouse is through this lobby. One elevator and one staircase," Tucker explained. "We've got them both locked down. Local watch suggested we establish our perimeter downstairs."

Vetch nodded. "And that elevator?"

Tucker pointed to a hallway at the back of the lobby. Around the corner was a solitary set of elevator doors, marked "Private".

Another constable was stationed in the elevator.

"Penthouse, Inspector?"

Vetch nodded, then turned to the doctor, "Unless you want to see something else first?"

Dr. Fell shook his head. "If I will wish to see anything else, it will be later."

The constable inserted a key into the panel and turned it, and the car rose.

The lobby of the penthouse was a small, clean room, outfitted in the vaguely modern style that mistakes clinical sterility for dignity and gives social visitors the impression that they have come to the dentist by mistake. The floor was polished gray marble, the walls stark white, and upon one wall was hung a series of what could be called paintings only as an act of charity. To Inspector Vetch they seemed to be dropcloths from a mechanics shop, spattered with oil and stretched onto frames.

Dr. Fell took two steps into the room and stopped. "Abide a moment," he said.

Vetch had expected this delay and nodded without comment.

From his inside jacket pocket the doctor retrieved a small leather-bound case and flipped it open expertly. Inside was a hypodermic syringe of his own design and a row of small glass vials. He extracted one vial and held it up to the light. The fluid inside was green, shot through with tiny threads of brilliant red. He considered the fluid.

"I've been adjusting the mixture," he said, still staring at the drifting threads. "I think my last batch of tigerberry was a bit off. The morouxe can't seem to grasp the concept of quality control, no matter what I pay them."

Dr. Fell shrugged and took out the syringe, then handed the case to Vetch, who held it gravely. The doctor fitted the vial into the syringe and injected himself, not in the cubital fossa of the arm, which might have been expected, but into the vein of his wrist.

He closed his eyes and stood very still for a moment. Then his skin seemed to ripple, like a flag in a high wind, as his muscles tensed and then relaxed. His lips parted and his breath sighed out.

When he opened his eyes again there was an intensity to them which had not been present before, a glimmering of what seemed a preternatural intellect. His thin face was more animated, a faint smile gave a mocking curl to his lips.

"My case," Dr. Fell said, and even his voice sounded different, more languorous and sensual.

Vetch offered the case. Dr. Fell replaced the syringe, then put the case back in his pocket. His movements were more fluid, his breathing quicker. Vetch had seen this transformation of his friend on numerous occasions, but it had never lost its power to both captivate and disturb him.

"Now," Dr. Fell said, anticipation on his features, "let's find us a murderer."

At the end of the lobby were ostentatious doors, set with panels of polished steel, which led directly into a large sitting room, the inhabitants looking uncomfortable in what were clearly last night's evening clothes. Seven people—four women and three men—were seated. Standing over them was a big, ugly man in a bad suit.

"They told me you were coming, Vetch," the big man said. He ignored Dr. Fell—didn't even seem to notice the little man.

The doctor spoke rapidly. "You would be Galgol. Let me guess, you found nothing of any consequence? Very well, you may leave."

Galgol gave the doctor a sharp glance then looked back at Vetch.

Vetch shrugged, looking uncomfortable. "We can take it from here."

Galgol offered a sheaf of papers to Vetch, then bent to retrieve a large case of black Bakelite, studded with dials and switches.

The doctor darted forward to snatch the papers from Galgol's hand. The sheets were printed with the complex lines of a thaumic flux graph, the Witchfinder's careful notations in black pen. Rapidly—too rapidly, it seemed, for him to be actually reading the dense notations—Dr. Fell scanned the sheets.

"As I expected," the doctor said absently, "some minor residuals, nothing recent, the traces of a few mystical toys and, oh, what's this?"

He scanned the still-seated crowd, and his eyes came to rest on one of the women, then looked back at the papers. "You've had a recent spell cast on you. Cosmetic, one assumes." His eyes flicked back to the woman, who was glaring at him, her arms folded over her chest. "Metabolic enhancement, am I right? Burning off the afternoon bonbons and crème de menthe, were we?"

He thrust the papers back at Galgol. "Oh, are you still here?" Dr. Fell asked.

Galgol hefted his case and stalked angrily towards the elevator lobby. Vetch took the papers from the doctor, folded them neatly, and stuck them in his jacket pocket.

The doctor glanced around the room, his bright eyes resting on each person in turn.

"Well," he decided, "since none of you appear to be dead, we'll have to continue this delightful conversation presently."

Vetch sighed almost imperceptibly and addressed the assembled guests. "If I could get some information from you, we'll get this sorted as quickly as possible." He removed a small notebook from his jacket.

Dr. Fell, meanwhile, sauntered down the hallway, whistling.

The penthouse was simple in design, a long central corridor with rooms to either side. The doctor glanced into each room as he passed it, stopping only when he saw the white-clad coroner's man.

"You have a cadaver for me, I believe?" he asked, his eyes bright.

The man nodded and gestured with a gloved hand. The room contained a large desk and several expensive leather chairs. Shelves covered two of the walls, supporting a collection of exotic artifacts from abroad. The doctor paused to study an empty display stand sitting between a lens of polished Ventrose crystal and an elaborately embroidered norn's prayer cloth.

The outer wall was glass, displaying a balcony. The doors had been forced, crudely and evidently in haste, as the glass of one of them was shattered.

On the balcony proper was a pair of chaise lounges. Upon one of those was a figure covered with a sheet.

The other coroner's deputy was waiting and pulled back the sheet. The body of a middle-aged man lay there, looking fat and soft. His neck had been raggedly cut and his torso was a mass of dried blood.

"You examined our friend here, one assumes?" Dr. Fell asked the deputy.

"He died from that cut," the white-clothed man said. "Likely between midnight and two, from the body temperature."

"The weapon?"

"This." It was an exotic looking knife, with a blade of some kind of yellowed ivory, shaped to end in a wicked hook, and an ornate handle wrapped in sharkskin.

The doctor looked without touching it. "Undine make. No doubt one of our victim's own souvenirs—I noticed the stand. You won't get any fingerprints from that handle—anything on the blade?"

"It was wiped clean."

Dr. Fell nodded. He bent to examine the body's arms. "No other wounds?"

"None. Just the slash on the throat."

"Didn't see it coming," Dr. Fell mused. "Murdered by a close friend. So many are—we should issue public health warnings on the danger of having friends."

"He'd have to have been, in any case," the deputy said. "No one else could have gotten to him."

Dr. Fell spared him a withering glance. "That remains to be seen."

The deputy bristled. "I'm just giving you the facts."

"It's a fact when I say it's a fact," Dr. Fell said. "Until I have directly observed it, it is a rumor."

Without giving the other a chance to reply, Dr. Fell went on, "Who smashed the door?"

"Mr. Manning and Mr. Poste," the other answered, tight-lipped. "Two of the gentlemen in the other room. They saw the deceased and broke the door to get to him, by their report. Near dawn, they say."

"And then called the authorities, too late for aid. They must have been seeking vengeance, then. Well, I shall endeavor to oblige them." The doctor glanced around the balcony. A heavy stone balustrade ran along the edge of the roof. In addition to the two chaise lounges, there was a small wrought iron table on which sat a bottle of dark wine, nearly empty, and an ashtray, quite full.

"I wish to speak to our inadequate Samaritans," Dr. Fell said and turned to leave the balcony, pausing only long enough to examine the lock on the now-broken doors. On his way out of the study he called over his shoulder, "You can remove the meat now, there's nothing more to be learned from it."

Returning to the sitting room, Dr. Fell looked at the seated persons, seeming to notice them for the first time.

"Introductions are in order," he said. "I am Linus Fell, as you all are no doubt aware. I have already met the gentleman outside. Who was he, by the way?"

Vetch answered quickly. "Cornelius Mordred. He's the owner of the penthouse and the host of last night's party."

Dr. Fell nodded quickly. "I believe I know the name. Banker or some such financial adventurer?"

"Investment banker, yes," Vetch said. "Rather more successful than most, as it

happens."

"And his widow would be...?" Dr. Fell asked.

Vetch grimaced at the crudeness of the question.

A young woman in a red velvet dress stood, a bit shakily. "I am Ambrosia Mordred."

"Condolences for your loss and all that. You may be seated."

She slumped back to her couch.

"Now if we can continue, please state your name for me, one at a time, and then perhaps we can get this all sorted?" Dr. Fell pointed.

"I am Elizabeth Tanner." The woman who stood was in her well-preserved middle-age. She was dressed in a suit of deep forest green, the jacket open over a white blouse secured with a black silk cravat, her skirt cut to emphasize her long legs. "And I must object to your insensitive manner. Have you no respect for grief?"

"None whatsoever," Dr. Fell replied. "The young man beside you?"

"This is Max—," she began, but the doctor cut her off.

"Let him answer me."

Mrs. Tanner sat back and crossed her arms.

The man who stood was scarcely more than a boy, and exceedingly handsome. His suit was dark and fine. "I am Maxwell Kent. I am Mrs. Tanner's secretary."

"Secretary," Dr. Fell mused. "Keeper of the secrets. What secrets do you keep for Mrs. Tanner?"

The young man's mouth tightened. "Her

social calendar," he said. "And certain aspects of her business affairs."

"I am sure that is all quite fascinating. Let us move along sharply. The corpulent gentleman next?"

The man so indicated got to his feet, leaning heavily on a stout oak cane worked with gold. "I am August Manning, of Manning & Goodstone. Perhaps you've heard of my firm?"

"I could scarcely have not," Dr. Fell remarked, "since you've plastered the city with your billboards. I must admit I've never had occasion to enter one of your shops, however. Your claim is that you sell everything, and I generally only go to market for one thing at a time."

His eyes went to the woman beside him.

"Tellus Manning," she said, standing. She was a bit younger than her husband, made up to look much younger. She was the woman he had singled out earlier as the source of the cosmetic magic. She looked at the doctor with undisguised loathing and sat back down.

"I admire your brevity," Dr. Fell said as he turned his attention to the final couple.

"Duke Poste," the thin man said, neglecting to rise. He was bearded and wore violet-tinted spectacles. "The playwright."

"Kay Poste," said the woman beside him. She was painfully thin, and her dress left most of her long limbs bare. Like her husband, she had remained seated.

"The playwright's wife," Dr. Fell remarked. "Third in a series, if memory serves."

Mrs. Poste glared.

Dr. Fell seemed unconcerned by the roomful of hateful stares. He smiled and rubbed his hands together. "Now, to the events of last night. It was a private party, I assume? Dinner followed by cognac and cigars—no, strike that, I smell neither. Dinner followed by tedious small talk. It requires a key to reach this floor. So privacy was assured, eh?"

Vetch spoke up. "In addition to the key, there is a switch on this floor that cuts power to the elevator. On the doorman's console is a light which shows when the power is on. The doorman is quite certain that it remained unlit all night."

"No doubt well-tipped by the late Mr. Mordred to be observant of such things," Dr. Fell nodded to himself. "We may take his testimony as genuine."

He paused and then continued, "The eight of you were here all night, and no one entered or left the floor—but wait, surely there are fire stairs?"

"The door to the stairwell is alarmed and rings a bell at the doorman's station, as well," Vetch said.

"To facilitate the invoking of a state of emergency," Dr. Fell observed. "For surely nothing else could induce the well-bred to climb down fourteen flights." He nodded, "What of the Gentle Folk?"

No one answered him, so he continued. "The kitchen?" He sighed. "The cabinets in the kitchen have pictographs on them, designed for use by Gentle Folk servants. But you don't have quarters for them, at least not on this floor. Did you have such servants here last night to assist with the party, and if so, where are they now?"

Mrs. Mordred spoke up then. "We have a service we use, but I only have Gentles for large parties. I did all the cooking and serving myself last night."

"Which would explain the dishes left in the sink," Dr. Fell said, nodding to himself. "You placed them there to ferment and congeal and rejoined your guests."

Mrs. Mordred opened her mouth and after a moment closed it again.

"Well, then, in the darkest hour of the night, Mr. Mordred was on his balcony, stargazing, one assumes, with the door secured from the balcony side. Somehow, despite that precaution, he met an untimely end. Even a cursory perusal of the wound makes it clear that it could not have been self-inflicted. Curious, that," Dr. Fell spoke softly, as if to himself.

He fell silent for a moment, then looked to August Manning. "It was you and Mr. Poste who broke open the door, yes? Can you relate that experience to me?"

Manning frowned. "Poste noticed the blood. He came and woke me. Together we forced the door."

Dr. Fell raised an eyebrow. "The portly and elderly grocery mogul rather than the fit and athletic Mr. Kent? Explain your reasoning, Mr. Poste?"

Poste seemed uncomfortable at the question. "I... know August well. He's been a sponsor of my work for years."

"In time of travail, you sought the familiar," Dr. Fell remarked. "Perfectly reasonable. And who telephoned the police?"

"I did," Mrs. Poste said. "I was closest to the phone."

"Which is where?" Dr. Fell asked.

"There are several instruments in the apartment," Vetch said. "She used the one in the hall, near the balcony."

"The call reached the station at...?" Dr. Fell asked.

"5:28," Vetch supplied.

"Only a few minutes past sunrise, then," Dr. Fell looked to Poste. "Is it your custom to arise so early? My impression has always been that thespians keep late hours, and I would have assumed that playwrights do as well."

"I worked through the night," Poste explained. "I frequently do, and Cornelius makes his study available to me on nights when I am here."

Dr. Fell nodded. "And then when rosy-fingered dawn crept through the windows, you arose from your labors to enjoy the view from the balcony, which is when you espied the deceased. Eminently logical."

He turned to face Manning again. "At which point he aroused you, in order to assist in the destruction of a fine set of glass doors. And also to alert his wife, of course, who had shared your bed."

Dr. Fell paused, smiling gently, but no one contradicted him. The silence in the room was cold and hard.

"Which makes one wonder where Mrs. Manning slept—" Dr. Fell began, but Tellus Manning leapt to her feet.

"I do not care for what you're implying!" she cried.

"Ah," Dr. Fell said mildly. "You were there as well. A bit crowded, I expect. One wonders why you did not call the police yourself. But, no, you would have gone to comfort the newly-minted widow. Your compassion does you credit."

Mrs. Manning stood and glared her hatred at him.

"Do sit, dear lady," Dr. Fell said. "The irregularity of your personal affairs, I care not at all about, but I have not yet eliminated you as a murderess. I will have you restrained if you cannot remain still."

Very carefully, she sat. Mr. Manning placed a hand on her shoulder, and she shrugged it off with a grimace.

"All this having been accomplished," Dr. Fell continued, "someone—Mrs. Poste, I expect, after her conversation with the authorities, woke Mrs. Tanner and Mr. Kent."

"Who slept in separate rooms," Mrs. Tanner said archly, "since you seem to care so much about that issue."

"Naturally," Dr. Fell agreed. "Keeping the boy on a starvation diet ensures he remains smitten with you."

Again a cold silence enveloped the room for an uncomfortable period. Vetch looked away from the assembled suspects, feeling ill at ease. Dr. Fell, however, smiled charmingly, looking as if he was having the time of his life.

"The critical question at this juncture is why all of you agreed to dine here last night, seeing as all of you—with the possible exception of Mrs. Mordred—clearly loathed the wretch," Dr. Fell mused.

Ambrosia Mordred exclaimed, "How can you say that? I loved my husband."

Dr. Fell nodded. "All of you without exception, then. The wonder is not why he was slain at the small hours of the night, but how he survived until that time."

He turned to face Mrs. Turner. "Your business is textiles, I believe? Import and wholesale. Each season, the new fashions owe much to your labor—which is not a compliment, by the way. How far in debt to Mr. Mordred are you, ma'am?"

Mrs. Turner stiffened her shoulders. "I do business with Mr. Mordred's banks, of course. As with others."

"As bad as all that, eh?" Dr. Fell raised an eyebrow. "Of course his demise won't erase your debts, but the resultant confusion will surely delay collection proceedings, if any had begun."

"I killed him!" Maxwell Kent announced suddenly, leaping to his feet. "I confess. He was a beast, an absolute beast, and I slaughtered him like a beast."

Dr. Fell turned his eyes to the boy. "And the matter of the locked door? Did you apport through it?"

"I climbed across the roof," Max said. "Once I cut his throat, I went over the roof and back into the window of my own room."

"No, you didn't," Dr. Fell said.

"I killed the bastard, I tell you!"

"No," Dr. Fell said mildly, "for if you had, you would have known that the doors were equipped with a spring latch. The real murderer simply stepped through and pulled the door shut behind him—or her—and it locked automatically."

"But—" the boy exclaimed.

"Sit." Dr. Fell's voice was firm. "Your

loyalty to your employer does you credit, but it is unnecessary. You need not confess to the crime in order to shield Mrs. Turner, because it is obvious that Mrs. Turner did not do it. The blow that severed Mr. Mordred's vital pipes was crude and brutal. Not the work of a former seamstress at all. Mrs. Turner, had you occasion to use a knife on a man, I would expect to see a neat incision."

Mrs. Turner stared at the doctor. "Should I thank you?" she asked.

"I wouldn't if I were you," Dr. Fell replied. "No, it was neither of you. You haven't the savagery, and your boy hasn't the brains."

Max started to speak, and the doctor cut him off. "My advice to you is to stick to lawful tasks when trying to impress members of the fair sex. Fetching boxes from high shelves, for example. That's something that I think you could do competently, and it allows you to display that trim figure."

Max began to rise, and Mrs. Turner put a hand on his shoulder. "Just ignore the man," she said. "He's not worth the effort."

"Young man, invest in a stepladder," Dr. Fell suggested, then grew more serious. "But you two were present at last night's dinner to ask a favor, undoubtedly an extension of Mrs. Turner's loan. I presume by your demeanor that it was granted, and hence you lack motive as well."

"Mr. Manning, on the other hand, would not have needed to ask for a loan." Dr. Fell turned his attention to the next pair. "In fact, the business went the other way. Your shops are doing quite well, and I imagine you function as a source of capital to the Mordred banks."

"That fact is well-known," Manning said. "I invest heavily in new businesses and Cornelius manages—managed—my investments."

"And yet you bore him no love," Dr. Fell said, as if working out a puzzle. "Don't bother to prevaricate, I see it written in the set of your muscles as plainly as if you'd had it printed on your billboards. You're glad he's dead, and your darling wife is even more so."

Tellus Manning gave a sharp intake of breath, but said nothing.

"Why does a man give money to a man he hates?" Dr. Fell mused. "Well, blackmail is the obvious answer. Granted, he was very good at delivering a return to his investors, but no man who routinely takes two women to his bed would value profit above self-respect. So, blackmail it is. Please, don't deny it, and for the sake of all that is holy don't confess it either. I don't care in the slightest what he had on you. It was enough that he was able to compel a steady stream of revenue, and that he has it no longer."

Dr. Fell paused and studied the room, staring not at the persons, but at the furnishings, the lights, the walls and ceiling of the room. He nodded to himself and turned back to Manning.

"I'd not trouble myself about any dead letter drops or other revenge from beyond the grave from Mr. Mordred, if I were you," Dr. Fell said. "Only frightened men make such precautions, and this is not the home of a frightened man."

Dr. Fell then turned to Mrs. Manning.

"You, my dear, are useless to me. You are an opera heroine, who would not dream of committing any atrocity without an audience. Should you ever murder anyone—and I don't recommend it, prison grays would ill-become you—I should not be needed to convict you. Save your simmering passion for the boudoir and your crimes against propriety."

"And now, the grieving widow," Dr. Fell said. "Pray, do not waste your crocodile tears on me, I shan't be moved, and you will need them for the press ere long."

He considered her in silence for a long moment. Then he said, "That dress is of an exquisite fabric, and the red suits you, but it is of a standard cut—not designed to specification. Other women might be at this very moment—well, not likely at this very moment, as it is an evening frock, but you grasp my meaning—wearing that design. A man such as Cornelius Mordred would not notice that, but a woman who had married a man like Cornelius Mordred would be very much aware of it. Thus, you wore that dress deliberately, which implies that it is from Mrs. Tanner's firm and you wore it to flatter her. The gold necklace at your throat is too heavy for the dress—too heavy for you, in fact. Thus, you wore that for your husband, who gave it to you. The heels on your delightful shoes are lower than the fashion; one assumes that you wore them knowing that there would be no servants allowed on this floor tonight and you would be doing the service yourself. You are, in all ways, turned out as the very soul of premeditation."

Dr. Fell looked down at the ground for a moment, then back at Mrs. Mordred. "Was this a premeditated crime? It does not appear so, but the acme of artifice is the appearance of spontaneity. You do have the motivation, after all. The man's death will cede you his wealth without the necessity of enduring his no doubt tiresome demands for comfort. A very clever woman might arrange for a house full of enemies and a locked room to confuse her own involvement in a crime. The question then becomes, are you a very clever woman?"

Dr. Fell looked at Mrs. Mordred and she looked coolly back, no expression on her face.

"You are not," Dr. Fell decided. "Or rather, you are not clever in wickedness. You have the curse of the fairest of your sex, that you have a genius that serves you only when doing good. You might have poisoned the brute—in fact, I admire your restraint in that you did not—but arranging this theater is quite beyond your powers."

Dr. Fell looked to the last two of the suspects.

"Mrs. Poste," he began, "theater is in your blood, I believe? You were an actress before you decided to cut out the theater owner and simply marry the playwright."

Kay Poste stared daggers at the doctor. "You, sir, are a monster."

Dr. Fell shrugged in acknowledgment. "A fact both true and irrelevant. I am an ugly and a necessary thing, like a toilet or tidewall. I am tolerated because I remove what is both ugly and unnecessary, such as murderers. Or murderesses. Are you one?"

"Why would I kill Mr. Mordred?" she hissed back.

"A dutiful wife might kill Mr. Mordred because he threatened her husband's livelihood," Dr. Fell said mildly. "But then, a dutiful wife would not become a member of another man's harem. If that was, in fact, the meaning of last night's arrangements. Perhaps it was the attentions of Mrs. Manning that you craved—in either event, it mitigates against having such great loyalty to your husband that you would commit murder on his behalf.

"Which leaves you, Mr. Poste," the doctor said, turning his attentions to the playwright. "Sadly, I can see no impediment to your hand holding the knife that let out the lifeblood of your patron. I do see—from having suffered through a number of your plays—multiple impediments to yours having been the brain that directed the strike.

"That will not matter to the courts, of course," Dr. Fell continued. "Should you choose to take the entire onus of this murder on your own shoulders, you may find it earns you a certain respect with your fellow felons on death row. I am given to believe that it is deemed integrity to conceal another's involvement in the crime that leads you to the gallows. You and I will know the truth, of course, but I am not obligated beyond discovering the villain of the piece."

Duke Poste leapt to his feet in a rage—a rage directed not at Dr. Fell, but to another. "You!" the playwright screamed, "You got me into this!"

The object of the playwright's ire sat solidly, without expression. "I did nothing. This is all your doing."

"The Hell it is," Poste cried. "It was your idea from the beginning. You set up this whole evening! Arrest him, not me. August Manning killed Mordred!"

"We'll arrest you both," Vetch said simply, "and sort it out at the station house. And the courts."

He picked up the house phone to call the detective stationed at the lobby desk.

In Inspector Vetch's car on the way back to the doctor's home, Dr. Fell looked out the window, watching the passersby on the sidewalk and humming to himself.

"Linus," Vetch said, an edge to his voice.

"Hmm?"

Vetch sighed. "Do you remember asking me to remind you of the dangers associated with prolonged mental acceleration?"

"Oh, you're right, of course," Dr. Fell said sourly. "My own personal mother hen. Whatever would I do without you."

He reached into his jacket pocket and removed his case. Moving with evident reluctance, he fitted a vial into his syringe. This vial was filled with a yellowish fluid. He held it up to the light, studying the liquid.

"Do you want me to pull over?" Vetch asked.

"No need," Dr. Fell said, and sighed. "It's a bit like a self-inflicted wound to the soul, you know."

Moving dexterously despite the movement of the car, he injected himself again, in the back of the hand. Then he closed his eyes and bent forward, like a man stricken

**WHEN AN EMPEROR TAKES
EVERYTHING FROM HIM
HE TAKES IT ALL BACK...AND MORE!**

AVAILABLE NOW AT AMAZON.COM

by a sudden illness. Vetch kept his eyes on the road, not looking at his companion. After a time he heard Dr. Fell speak.

"I was quite horrible, wasn't I?" the doctor's voice was soft and his cadence slow, the voice of a man emerging from a nightmare.

"No worse than usual, Linus," Vetch said.

"That's no comfort," the doctor said. "Not to me. Was it worth it?"

"We broke the case," Vetch answered. "Don't know that we could have, apart from you."

"I suppose that's something," the doctor said softly. "The gallows is always hungry, eh?"

"Linus, what you do is a great service to the city. I know it costs you, and believe me when I say that on the day you decide to put away your chemicals and be no more than an ordinary man, no one will support you more than I."

"But it is not this day," the doctor said in a near whisper. "Please, don't pay attention to me just now. My head aches, and it feels like I've been dragged behind a garbage truck. It will pass."

They had reached the doctor's townhouse. Vetch pulled in to the curb. "Do you want me to stay?"

The doctor shook his head and opened the car door. "No, best to be alone. I'll gorge myself on rare beef and stout; I'll get past this. Until next time."

Vetch looked solemnly at his friend. "Until next time."

Misha Burnett is a self-educated and self-published author who draws upon his professional background in the security and maintenance fields to bring a solid sense of reality to his fantastic tales. He is the creator of The Book Of Lost Doors series of novels; Catskinner's Book, Cannibal Hearts, The Worms Of Heaven, and Gingerbread Wolves, available on Amazon.

Crying in the Salt House

By B. MORRIS ALLEN

In the desert stands a house made entirely of salt! On the flats, slaves endure the travails of mining and collecting the salt, but worse still are those who suffer the machinations of the mad-man who has built his manse in the wastes!

The Salt House is built on tears, not of them. That is only a little joke the Bracque like to play. They tell visitors that the blocks of pure, clear salt are the crystallized tears of children, and the rougher, grayer stones are the tears of the parents who lost them.

It is not true. Had it been, we should all have wandered the halls with little vials strapped to our faces, and the House would be much larger than it is.

The visitors believe, because they look for romance, and because they are disappointed. They come from far away, and they find only a squat gray house with slumping walls of stone. It is not the limpid, lucent castle they found in their heads. Some of them go away without seeing inside. They are content with the tawdry, gaudy mock-ups put up by the Bracque, accurate in every notion, incorrect in every detail.

It is true that the House is no beauty. It stands on the barren salt pan where once a sea pooled shallow among low hills and far mountains. The land is parched and harsh, and even the Bracque live on the fringes, at the mouths of creeks that once were rivers, before the land lifted and shifted, before the

sea drained dry. Now all that is left is the flat seabed, crusted with salt to a child's waist height. I know, for I have stood in it.

Nothing lives on the salt. It is why *he* was sent here from the green cities of the south. They condemned him to die slow and lonely, because they had not the will to kill him quickly. Instead of dying, he built the House. He is a resourceful man, our master, and a stubborn one. It will stand him in good stead.

The salt of the seabed is not suited for building. It is thick but friable, and it melts in the rain. The House is built instead of evaporite stones from the northern hills, mined by free Bracque and by prisoners from the south. The stones are dark and dreary, with streaks of white running down their faces from moisture. They melt also, but more slowly, so that the roofs and crenels of the House are rounded and tired, but whole.

The Bracque say he deliberately built the House from mined salts as a gesture to his enemies. They say much and know little. The master is a man of the future, a man of clear vision. He does not think of the south, except in terms of business.

When I first came to the salt, I was too young to think, except of the present. My father had been fined and then sentenced for improper solicitation, which means turning down the advances of the nobility. "It is noble to think always of yourself," he told me. I did not know the meaning of irony at the time.

In fact, it is in the nature of people to think always of themselves. It is the essence of survival, I think. Looking beyond oneself is a risk. Our master looked deeper and further than most, and see him now. They come to see him every day.

My father died in the mines. It is a slow death, and painful, choking in the cold salt grime, but it seemed rapid to me. One day, he left and told me to wait. Another day, they came to tell me he had died and that I had become a ward of the master. Nothing changed, except that after another year I ceased to wait.

Waiting is an art we know much of, here in the salt—waiting for rain, for revenge, for release. We wait still, spinning around the House, like the world spinning on its axis, leaning sometimes one way, sometimes another, but never changing position. The master waits with us, and often I think he is the only one who knows what for. Perhaps we only wait for him to tell us.

When he was exiled, he used the last of his influence to purchase a salt license, a right to provide the pure, fine salt that sparkles like diamond across southern tables and lies like dust upon their dishes.

We scoop it up with shovels in the salt pan, deep in the interior, where the Bracque have not fouled it with their wastes and their fires. When I came to the House, I worked as a holder, holding open the mouths of the soft, tightly woven fine-sacks for a filler to shovel salt dust into. It is easy work, but hard on the body. Many of the children die of it, never learning how to guard their eyes and noses, and not least the ears.

"Take off your shirt," my filler told me, on my first morning. I did because though my father had warned me against disrobing, he had also warned me what would come if I fought against authority. "Always choose the lesser of two evils," he had told me. It is not so easy a choice as it seems.

"Small, aren't you?" the filler, Rula, asked, and indeed her lean form towered above me, runnels of sweat already etched into a layer of salt along knotted muscle, though her torso was closely covered. "You'll grow." She took my shirt from me and tore strips from its tail. I had no other, nothing in fact but loose trousers I wore with a string to hold them up. "Here," she said, giving me back a tatter of cloth.

I took the remains of my shirt, put my arms through it, and let the yoke settle. My belly was cool where the shirt ended in ragged threads. "Now these," she said, and plugged my ears with cloth when I stared at her in bafflement. "And the nose. And around the eyes." She thrust a soft sack into my hands, showed me how to hold it open. "Never," she said, "never open your eyes until I say so." And for years I did not, though within two years I was a filler myself, and Rula was gone to the House. It is easiest, sometimes, to have a reason for not seeing.

As a holder and filler, I did not live in the House itself. I lived with Rula and the other prisoners' children in a Bracque encampment at the edge of the seabed. The Bracque were foul and coarse, but they worked hard enough when they cared to. Near as many of them died in the master's mines as did prisoners, though they were better paid. Minding children was easy work in comparison. Besides, where would we go, with seabed to the north and west, rocks to the east, and nothing but civilization to the south?

A Bracque matron named Erna would march us to the salt pit every day and set us to work. Occasionally, a boy or girl would be tasked to fetch more fine-sacks, or the coarser bags we packed those into, or a crew would be set to hauling a wagonload south to the encampment. Those walk-tasks were coveted assignments, and Erna liked to see us scuffle for them. The walk-work was hard; the salt tore at our toughened feet, and the wagon traces sank into our muscles like wire, but out in the open, we could breath. "The air is only ten-percent salt," walkers would joke, an improvement on the clouds of salt that surrounded fillers and holders like a caustic mist.

Eventually, I graduated to filler, alongside Rula. We could not talk during the day, for if you opened your mouth, the salt would come in, and then you would cough, and breathe in more, and you would collapse there in the salt, and the holders would be made to drag you out.

We talked at night in the camp, when it was too dark to dig. The Bracque had a little stream they used for drinking water, and Rula insisted we bathe in it every week. We would walk up into the hills a little, where a low ridge hid the Bracque's low huts and our own shabby lean-tos. There Rula would insist I turn my back and keep guard. I earned my keep, for though she was too young to have any curves, there were always those wanting to look, or to tell lies about what we did there together. It is a strange thing that so many of us seek out only what is forbidden and turn away from what is before us every day.

One night, as I took my turn bathing, and Rula watched over me, she told me that she had reasoned out the way of Erna and her tasks. "She does not choose the one who fights the best, but the roughest, the most desperate. The most grateful." And once a week, the most attractive; that was understood, but Rula was too gawky to be chosen for sex.

"Erna is a bully," she said, and since coming to the salt, I had learned something of bullying. Bullying is to take something from someone so that they hurt, not because you want it. I think we are all the bully at times. "When next there is a walk-task," Rula said, "make a fuss. Pretend to fight me, but I will let you win. Then Erna will choose you, because you are small and you have beaten me. You must try to cry when we fight." We all cried all the time from the salt, as if it were the only way to rid our bodies of an excess of the stuff.

"I will not cry if you do not hit me," I said, to show tough, because Rula was a hard girl, and she would not cry from only frustration or loss.

"Oh, I will hit you. And you must hit me as well." She stopped her talk to look and listen for no one there. "But you must make sure not to hit me here." She gestured toward her midriff, where ribs joined belly.

"I will not hit you anywhere," I said, for Rula was my one protector, and if I hit her, whom would I turn to?

"No, you must. I insist on it, boy," and she smiled to play the noble with me. "Only not here. I have…I have an injury here. A growth of sorts." I could see that it hurt her, and I was surprised that she hid the pain so well, digging in the salt. "But you must wrestle with me, and hit me as if you were my brother. Are we agreed?"

I agreed, though I had no brothers, and no sisters either, and I did not know how to hit them.

On the next task day, Rula and I put on a good performance, and she fetched up with a bloody nose, crying for real from the pain of the salt we had rolled in. I, triumphant, ignored the ache in my belly where Rula's elbow had dug in hard, and stood up for Erna to call me. In my nervous excitement, I forgot to cry, and I sometimes wonder how things might have been different had I been less hard.

Erna did not call my name. I have never been sure whether she saw through Rula's childish ploy, or whether, true to her nature, Erna simply chose to flaunt her power by defying expectations. In either case, I learned an important lesson about subtlety. She called instead to Rula, where she knelt in the white salt dust, pretending defeat. Rula flicked her eyes sideways to me, and I shrugged. The ploy had worked, and if Rula were the one to benefit from her own idea, that was surely right.

She never came back. Often in life, we learn the important matters too late. Before Rula, I never had a friend that I can recall. Not until I lost her did I know that she was a friend to me and more, and the knowledge set in my heart a pang that has never quite left it.

After two weeks, I bathed by myself, and cut my hair with a borrowed knife, and caught Erna's eye. I learned, at the expense of a tedious evening licking salt off the more noisome portions of her spare figure, that Rula had been taken into the Salt House, to serve there.

When my service to Erna was done, I rose in the moonlight and walked to the edge of the seabed. There, across the flat, white plain, the House swelled, a small, dark protuberance like the nipple on Erna's breast. My first imagination of Rula in the house is thus always tangled with Erna's gross desire. It is a matter of some frustration to me.

I went to the House myself within the year. My night with Erna paid also for one trip to collect sacks, and the others I won by chance. I let Erna bully me without complaint, and she lost the pleasure in it.

On my first visit, I came no nearer to the House than its storeroom, a squat gray extrusion of evaporite along the House's northern face. To the west of the House, a bed of flat tiles held a foul green liquid. It smelled of sewage, and so the storesgirl confirmed it to be.

"It has to go somewhere," she said. "At least here it dries and blows away." She wore tunic and trousers that came close to fitting, but she was a greasy, slovenly type, for all the fancy clothing.

"Never mind," I replied, and then, with as much confidence as I could muster, "Do you know Rula? Is she here? Is she well?"

Her eyes widened at the name. "I must go."

I grabbed her by the arm, greatly daring, for she was easily twice my age, and large with it.

"Let me go," she cried, and batted away my arms. I grabbed her again, as it was clear she knew something of Rula, and I meant to have it out of her if I had to hit her. "Let me go," she cried, and set her knee in my groin. It would have hurt me more in a few years, but it was bad enough, and I had only the will to grasp her ankles from where I lay on the salt. She kicked and stomped, but I held on to her as she shuffled toward the storeroom.

"Tell me," I cried, getting my breath back at last.

"What's this?" An old man of fifty or more, thin like sticks held together by clay, had emerged from the House. "Piro! Explain yourself. And you, boy, get up."

"He grabbed me, Nerk," she muttered. "And would not let go. He has gone wild, out in the ... out there."

"Are you wild, boy? So wild that you must be dragged on the salt rather than walk?" He jerked his head to Piro, and she slunk back toward the door.

"Well, boy? If you would enter the storeroom, you must answer to me, or I am no storesman, and as I am Nerk, and Nerk is a storesman, I must be one."

I had difficulty following his talk, but I covered it in climbing up from the salt and bowing to him. "My apologies, storesman Nerk," for so I thought him to be. "I sought only to learn the whereabouts of my friend, Rula, who came here some weeks since."

"Ah, Rula. And you are her friend, you say?"

"I am." Though it seemed a troublesome thing to be, I stood by it, for that is what friendship is for, and I had little else.

"A dedicated one, it seems. Well, I shall keep my eye on you. In any case, yes, she is here. A scrappy young thing, much like yourself, perhaps. So perhaps she will serve, in time. Or perhaps not." A shadow crossed his taut face, and he smiled it away. "We shall see. Indeed, we shall. But now, go your way, boy, and leave our Piro here alone."

And so I left, smelling the House's foul stench all the way back to the salt pit, for the wind had changed, and it bore with it my wonder at the House's strained atmosphere, but also my satisfaction, for it seemed Rula had made a mark for herself already.

My next few months in the salt pit taught me little. I filled sacks, avoided bullies, and kept happy knowing that Rula had found a place in the House. On occasion, Erna assigned me a walk-task, more from boredom than purpose, for I did nothing to gain her attention. On every visit to the House, I asked for Rula, and on every occasion, Nerk came out to eye me and to tell me she was well.

On my fourth trip to the House, Nerk told me to stay. He put me to work in the sack room, sewing the coarse bags that held the fine-sacks of salt powder.

"It's all you're good for," he said. "Show me your hands." I held out fingers cracked and callused by three years of living and shoveling salt. "As I thought. Maybe in a month or two, we can set you on the fine work. Or not. You've a look about you."

I looked about me. The exterior of the Salt House had been gray and dark, but for windows of stacked, translucent blocks. On the inside, the House lived up to its name. Save for pillars of light gray evaporite, the walls and floor and ceiling, were salt, as indeed was every surface. Not the dusty, brittle salt of the seabed, but blocks of hand-smoothed white and gray, veined in places with yellow, blue, and purple that I had never, in my years on the salt pan, imagined.

I learned with time that the purity of the salt rose with the level of the house, so that the highest floor, where the master worked, was built of blocks transparent as ice, and just as smooth. Here in the bowels of the House, wondrous as it seemed to me, were the dregs of the mine, the blocks just salt enough to merit the term.

I sat on the salt block floor, looking at these wonders, and wishing for someone to talk to about it. "Where is Rula?" I blurted to Nerk, as he turned from showing me the spot under a shelf where I was to sleep with the other sewers.

"Never you mind," he said shortly, and took me off to show me the other sewer. "We drain off the liquid here, see, let it out through these pipes. Left for west, right for east, depending on how the wind's blowing. Evaporates right away, it does, and the residue blows off across the salt pan. The solid stuff we put in a wagon, haul it out to the Bracque. They put it on their food or something."

It was all made of salt. Even the pipes and the cesspit, foul as they were, were made of ducts and blocks of grey evaporite.

"Does it not melt?"

"Course it does, eventually. This evaporite, stuff, though, it's not regular salt. Probably mostly rock, I guess. Takes a while to leak. When it does, though, that's a task, replacing all this. More often upstairs, of course. Do that pretty often. More true salt up there."

I worked in the storeroom for half a year. My fingers caught on the rough fabric of the canvas bags, and my thick-callused fingers fumbled with needle and thread, until Nerk despaired of teaching me to sew and set me to polishing floors instead. I wandered the lower floors with a small bucket and a soft cloth, wiping up the dust that constant foot traffic wore off the salt slabs, and cleaning my rag in water that slowly turned to brine. After an hour, my hands would tremble at the thought of one more rinse, one more wring that would work the salt into tiny cracks in my hands that would never close. By the end of the day, the tears would come, and leave their salt in the cracks along my cheeks and mouth. At that, I had more access to water than most, and I washed with it as well as I was able before starting my morning rounds. The water was already fourth hand by then, having been used by Nerk, and the chamberlain, and perhaps a guest or even the master before that. During a long day in the salt pit, I would have drunk it without question. Here in the Stone House, we had water enough for drinking and bathing both, some of us. It warmed me to think that Rula, too, could bathe daily, wherever she might be in the upper ranges of the House.

It was not for want of trying that I did not find her. For all its beauty, the House was oppressive, its still interior a cold contrast to the dusty chaos of the salt pit. Despite the cleaner air, it was almost as silent. Among the servants, we seldom spoke, and with each new arrival to a room, talk paused while all evaluated what had been said, and what might have been heard. I could not tell, at first, what subjects to avoid. It was only with time that I understood the fear was not of any subject, but of being noticed at all. By the time I knew this, I had already caught Nerk's eye, though no ill seemed to come of it.

In the storerooms, for there were more than one, we worked at our menial tasks, occasionally graduating to larger positions. Like me, the other children had no family and no thought beyond their daily work. Unlike me, Nerk paid them no special attention. "You've a look about you," he would say, especially when I pressed him about Rula. The children knew no more. "Gone in the salt," was all they would say of her. To a boy surrounded by salt, that meant little.

I used my cleaning tasks to search her out, walking near-invisibly into the guest areas, and more noticed into those used by servants. It was in the kitchen I had my first clue. There was a boy there not much older than me. He seemed friendly as he darted here and there for spices and provender. He was a striking child, with sandy skin and hair a thick, wild tangle of tight brown curls. One day, he let fall a chunk of brown crystal and mimed putting it in his mouth.

I did not need for salt, but it was a small cost for a kindly smile in that sad house, and I complied. I had never tasted sugar before. I savored the memory that evening, and all the next day, and the week after, going so far as to surreptitiously lick some of the browner floor stones. They were salt.

When I next had a chance to enter the kitchen with my rag, I asked after my new friend. "In the salt," was all he said, and the usually quiet kitchen stilled further until I left.

"It's a price," Nerk told me that evening. He shifted his feet as he sat in the storeroom. His gaze, so often sharp and penetrating, had become obtuse and vague, eyes shifting from shelf to shelf around the room. "It's a price, for what we have, what we all have." His eyes flicked to me momentarily. "And we all pay. Remember that. We all pay the price, one way or another." He would say no more.

Nerk set me to carrying messages and small bundles of supplies, so that I traveled a broader reach within the House, and even spoke on occasion to the upper servants.

The task came with clothes that fit, a shirt and trousers of barely-patched white cotton. I walked straight and proud and blind in my finery while the other low-servants slunk beside the walls. Pride is like the sun shining in your eye. The more you have, the brighter your path appears, and the fewer of its pitfalls you see.

After several months, my kitchen friend was back. I stopped short when I passed one day, to see him somberly chopping a row of carrots. I slipped through the door and smiled.

"Hello," I said, as he continued to chop.

He nodded. His face was the same gold hue as before, but lacked for sparkle, for vivacity.

"You're back," I added. "From the salt." Whatever that might be.

If his face had been still before, now it was flat as the salt pan outside, his eyes as dead as the fish we sometimes found in the bottom layers of the pit. He turned his white, staring gaze on me, then turned away, sweeping carrots into a heavy bowl. A cook ushered me out.

I had no chance to press Nerk for information in the next days, but the incident rekindled my search for Rula's whereabouts, for it meant one could come 'out of the salt' as well as going into it.

Nerk's tasks for me became more numerous and more trivial, sending me frequently to the upper levels of the House. One day, after I had delivered her an inconsequential message about a shortage of capers, the chamberlain laid a hand on my shoulder. She smelled nice, or perhaps only familiar, after so many days of using her old bathwater.

"You had a friend."

Here was an unexpected stroke of luck, and I was not shy to take advantage. "Ma'am. Rula, ma'am. Rula was my friend. She went into the salt." I said the phrase not as I had heard it, with flat fatalism, but with eagerness and optimism. She had gone in, and perhaps she had come out.

The chamberlain looked at me, seemingly more concerned with my demeanour than with my words. I waited expectantly.

"The master will see you," she said.

Until now, the master had been a distant, almost fancied figure in the House, so distant from the concerns of a storesboy that I had never troubled even to imagine him as more than a vague figure in white robes. I stared at the woman, mouth open to protest, except that storesboys did not protest orders from anyone at all, let alone the chamberlain herself.

"Close your mouth. Follow me." She turned, and I followed dumb down hallways of translucent white and pink that grew clearer and finer as we climbed toward the heart of the House. The master himself would tell me about Rula! Perhaps she had caught his eye, become a serving-maid, or even a concubine. Even modest Rula would not turn down such an opportunity, I felt sure.

I barely noted the beauty of the chambers we passed through, the delicate swirls of colour laid by sunshine and salt that we walked through as casually as mirages. I built up my own visions of the welcome

Rula would give me, of the warm, tolerant look of the master as he witnessed our reunion, allowed us to hug and hold hands in the warm sanctuary of his presence chamber. As he, why not, served us fresh water with his own hands.

Most of us are fools most of the time. There are many kinds: those who fool themselves, those who are fooled by others, those who are ignorant. All are fools the same, but the most foolish are those who close their eyes and expect the truth to be other than what they see plainly before them.

I spent four years in the salt. Longer than any before me, and still longer than any since. Longer than my kitchen friend, and longer by far than Rula.

The master never called it the salt. He called it the Transcendence. I called it many things, but never that.

The salt is a chamber, perfectly cubical, with walls made of the purest, clearest salt blocks, cut so smooth and joined so fine that it is like standing in open air, held up only by an intangible net of faintest white. We trust most what we see, when we bother to see it, but an invisible cage is still a cage.

My prison chamber stood free in the center of the master's parlor near the top of the house, with his study directly below, and the roof walk above. It was furnished with a bed of fine salt crystals, a thick basin of brine, and a privy built of the same clear salt as the walls. Though they had stripped my clothing from me as they lowered me into the chamber from the roof, it was warm enough. I did not notice it, for my attention was taken with tears and pleading.

On the fifth day, I tried violence, and it served no better than pleas. Salt, even in purest form, is rock, and rock is stronger than flesh. I soaked my wounds in salt water and cried for pain and shame.

After ten days, I tried to carve my way out with urine, but my urine was already so concentrated as to be little more than a spurt, and so foul-smelling that the smell kept me awake. When my feeble urine-cut in one block grew to a thumb-joint in depth, they replaced the block. I substituted brine from the basin, sprayed from my parched mouth, but it simply pooled on the floor, and the master shut off the flow until the pool had dried into a grey, unhealthy crust.

On all sides of the chamber, at different heights, little holes were bored through the salt, so that he could hear me, and I him. Throughout the day, the master spoke to me.

"Salt, given time and pressure, becomes a rheid. It looks like stone, but it acts like liquid. It transforms itself, transcends its limitations. It can shape itself to fit its surroundings, to escape rigid limits, and become more. More than itself, but without losing its own identity."

He watched me, as he worked, as he slept, as he took his morning walks on the roof above. There was no time that I felt unobserved, free to do the small things we all like to think are private, to pick my nose or scratch my groin. It was no great loss. There had been little privacy among the Bracque but what Rula found.

He would not speak of Rula, though I asked, demanded, insisted with all my youthful anger.

"You will see her one day," was all he said. "She is waiting for you."

After a month, my spirits were lower than they had been since I first came from the salt pit. My fists, torn by battering against crystal walls, stung with every move, every surface they touched. They coated themselves with salt at every bedtime, sluiced it away with every bath. I tried sleeping on the floor, but it was so hard I got no rest. I tried going without bathing, but he stopped providing water—clean water, the water I needed to live.

"You must be clean," he said. "Free of all encumbrance to transcendence."

I fouled the floor, but again he shut off the water, until at last I washed the cell clean. He watched the dirt pour down through the salt pipes, then gave me a small block of coarse gray salt. I scrubbed off layers of floor until only smooth crystal remained and he turned the stopcock and clean water returned.

My joints and muscles hurt for a time, so starved of moisture were they from the constant coating of salt. They had done the same in the salt pit; I had survived there, and I could survive here.

He watched me sleep, eat, cry, piss, shit. He watched my evacuations as they slid slowly down the salt pipes through his bedroom. I thought at first it gave him pleasure, but it did not. It was only data that he noted carefully in his logs.

"It is a question of transparency, you see. Transparency leads to transcendence. That is my hypothesis. It is true of salt, of glass,

of water. Why should it not be true of people?"

I laughed in his face. "If I starve myself, I will be so thin you will not see me. Then you will see me transcend for a certainty."

He only shook his head. "Not so, not so. I have seen it tried. Starvation leads only to death. It is not transcendence—far from it." He smiled, stretching the skin across the tight planes of his face. "It is not physical transparency that is important. It is a transparency of the spirit. When your mind is as transparent as this salt, then, you will be closer to transcendence."

I wanted to strike the clear blocks between us, to reach through shattered salt to close my hands around his throat. Yet my hands hurt, and I had proven already that the salt was proof against my strength. I tried, instead, to wound him with words.

"I see through you already. Perhaps you will transcend before me. Or die. As you like." It was little enough, and in fact, I had no real grasp of his purpose, though he had explained it quite sincerely.

"You may be right. We must always acknowledge possibility. However, I lack the second ingredient—not only transparency, but pressure. Salt reforms itself under pressure, and over time. Once we have determined the parameters of pressure and transparency for humans, then you will see me transform indeed, and welcome."

We were not always alone, the master and I. He had visitors, who attempted to ignore me, and the servants entered whether the master was there or not. They peered at me surreptitiously, as they tidied, stocked, and cleaned, but affected not to see or hear me. Once Nerk climbed up to us, reporting on an infestation of salt-lice in the food-stores. He looked everywhere but towards my cell, even when the master came to stand before me, and I made rude gestures behind his back. Nerk, brave man, only mumbled to the floor, and fled before his report was fairly finished.

"You see," said the master, when the storesman had gone, "already you begin. You exert your own pressure, beyond the bounds of your small chamber. I'm pleased. It's pressure, remember, that aids the transformation. Enough pressure, and a person will do anything. Most will fracture, like your two friends before you, but some, in just the right circumstances, they will transcend, will become more than they are. I'm sure of it."

Only the chamberlain seemed to recognize my presence, nodding to me each morning when she arrived for conference with the master over dried fruit and water. Her expression did not change, whether I was clean or covered in filth. She only nodded, sat, and served out the food before listing the day's problems.

Piro came on a regular basis, the slattern who had first greeted me at the House. She was cleaner now, but no more prepossessing. She did her cleaning work quickly, and looked on me with such a mix of relief and fear that I almost pitied her. Instead, I pleaded with her, insulted her, begged her, reviled her. The result was the same; she rushed through her work, leaving streaks of dust across the tables, crumbs of food in the corner. In the end she came no more, replaced by a stolid boy who saw me but made it clear he did not care.

I criticized Piro's work to the master, suggested that a period of transcendence might do her good.

"Oh no," he laughed. "We must start with good material. Piro will never transform. In fact, she has already left the House." He shrugged. "She reached maturity, and the payments stopped." For, as he explained to me, he received payments for support of all children to whom he acted as warden. I grew angrier than before with Piro, who had escaped so easily, but also hopeful, for the news suggested that even this imprisonment must have an end, if only I could survive it. Because I still had not opened my eyes, it took me longer to see the true lesson, which was that Piro had been wiser than me, that the master himself had seen no further than her slovenly garb and mien.

I had hoped to be set free at the four-month mark, as the kitchen boy had been. Already, I had forgotten my friend's looks, all memories merging into the same long, angular face, with its perpetual rash along the jaw where salt irritated skin scraped raw by a razor, no matter how gently held.

"It is a travesty," the master called up to me every day as he shaved. "But a beard is so hot in this climate, and it catches the salt. Not a worry for you, of course. Not for some time yet."

While I could hardly recall the boy's features, I had held tight to his period of incarceration. Four months. He had held out for four months, and I, who had survived the salt pits, could do no less. But four months went by without change, and then eight.

After a year, the master held a little celebration, he with a carafe of scarlet fruit juice, me with a salt glass of water. As always, I drank it quickly, before it could lose its purity to the salt.

He shook his head. "You must learn to savor these moments. You are, as of today, my best experiment, if not quite a result. It comes of the good raw materials, I believe." He held up his glass to me and sipped. "You have promise, real promise. I think we can go further with you. Already, you begin to see through me." He winked. "That bodes well."

When I asked about release, he tsked and shook his head. "Transcendence," he reminded me gently. "Transcendence is our goal. Do you feel you have transcended?" He shook his head. "Of course not. But you can. I feel it in you. I see it in your skin as it begins to glow." My skin glowed only with a sheen of sweat that streaked the salt away. Beneath, my skin was the same dull beige that it had always been.

After the first year, there was a period of blankness. I ate, I shat, I slept. I stared into nothingness. I thought as little as I was able, and with practice that was considerable. I believe I went days without a conscious thought, perhaps even weeks or months. I did the minimum to stay alive, to persist, to endure. Yet I have a restless spirit, and even in this condition my mind eventually reawakened.

"You're back," he said, one day, from his desk by the big salt window. And though I had gone nowhere, I laughed. It was true. I had retreated, and found no place to retreat to. In escaping my escape, I found myself back at the start, back in my cell.

"Still hope, then," he added. "Your kitchen friend did the same, much sooner, and I let him go. I see now that it was premature. Or perhaps it's the raw material again."

When I was sure the master still had no intent to let me out, I set to a truly thorough exploration. The walls were more visible to me now, my eyes more accustomed to their faint imperfections, their joins and cracks. But now I searched also with my fingers, aiming to touch every portion of the cell that I could reach. I found uncounted flaws—depressions, chips, rough spots, smooth ones, even, under the bed, deliberate scratches. I passed these over at first, my fingers moving on mechanically before my mind could perform its slow analysis. When I finally awoke to the import of these regular lines, I passed my hands back over them, with a surreptitious glance at the master, who fussed with paperwork under an oil lamp.

R – U – L – A. Rula! I probed eagerly for more, for some message from the past, but this was all. I searched feverishly across the entire underside of the bed, climbing under it entirely, searching with eyes as well as my fingers. I went so far as to lick the entire surface, hoping to catch some sign too faint for hard fingers to discern. There was nothing.

"You've found it, have you?" The master

stood outside the wall, watching intently. "I had to teach her the letters. She wasn't as lucky as you in your choice of parents."

I had little enough literacy, and it had not occurred to me that anyone could have less. What did it mean that he had taught her to write her name? I had no doubt that he had. For all his faults, the master never lied to me.

"She was more delicate than you, I'm afraid. It was a lesson for me to look less on the outside than the inside. Your friend didn't know that. She felt the need to leave her mark, and I let her do so."

This physical sign, this direct evidence of Rula's precedence in the salt, heartened me. Rula's mark on the salt was no more than faint scratches, but her trace on me was indelible.

From then on, I did not look back. I lived, I listened, I learned. The master spoke to me of his business, and I saw for myself the meetings he took, the furtive, shadowed figures so uneasy in his transparent house. I took it upon myself to distress them more, noting which looked upon my naked figure with distaste, and which with longing. After a time, the master began discussing their reactions with me.

"Well done. She could hardly keep herself from looking at you, especially when you began to cry, there in the corner. She signed with hardly a look, and I got a far better rate for the prisoners than I dared hope for."

I learned quickly that the master was paid for everything. Money always flowed his way, whether payment for care of pris-

oners, or for the rock salt they mined, or support payments for the prisoners' children, or for the fine salt they dug in turn. He received payments even for me, and would do so for years, he told me.

"You're my ward, you see? And don't I ward you well?" His laugh was a deep, booming tone that failed to match his lanky frame. "And your friend even better."

When he showed Rula to me, on my two year anniversary in the salt, I was unsurprised. She looked peaceful as he brushed tight-packed salt from her face. Dehydration had stretched her mouth into a rictus that mocked happiness, but her eyes, shrunken and sunk, seemed calm.

"I had to marinate her first, you see? It's important that the salt enter the tissues quickly and thoroughly. She had already opened one artery, of course, and I was able to flush the rest of the blood from the system quickly. The organs were more difficult, and I had to remove the intestines completely. Still, a year in strong brine, and then packed in fine salt, and it's not too bad, is it?"

Her young body looked frail, under its powder of salt, the joints seeming swollen on withered limbs. Across her ribs, an extra pair of tiny limbs dangled loose, one arm, one leg, like a child climbing slowly out or in above the devastation of her belly.

"Interesting, aren't they? You get that, sometimes, especially in some regions. It's the result of one twin eating the other, I believe, but not finishing the job. Your friend was quite sensitive about it."

I imagined hard, proud, private Rula,

exposed here for the master's observation, imagined her sitting in one corner or another, trying without success to hide her secret, the secret she had kept from me and from the Bracque, even there in the closeness of the salt pit. I pictured her succumbing to despair at last, forced to turn to her tormentor to ask even for the means to leave a mark, a sign of her own sad existence.

The salt had changed me as well, left me with a surface hard and sleek and impervious. I polished away my tears before they could disturb the glaze of my exterior, mar me and show the master more than a pale reflection of his self. I asked about preservation techniques, and about the uses of salt, and about transformation.

"Oh, you're getting on, you are. You'd make a fine assistant if I did not have other uses for you." Yet the skin flushed dark across his rash, and I could tell that for all his easy way, he was disturbed by the failure of his scheme.

He seemed to lose heart when even the sight of Rula failed to make me transform. He turned his attention briefly to other, more extreme means.

"We must work with the materials at hand, after all, and salt is what we have in plenty. Salt not only transforms itself, but is transformative of others, can we only find how to apply it." His attempts were grotesque, and there were days I felt happier inside my salt chamber than without. More and more of the servants found ways to leave the House, whether at maturity or not. The Bracque brought some back, but not many. Even the Bracque have their limits, and they made clear they found the master's work distasteful. After a time, he gave it up, though he kept Rula on display for me next to my chamber, and I watched as her flesh slowly shrank, and a faint pink slurry formed at the bottom of her box, until at last she seemed to float above a slab of marble.

It was two more years before I convinced the master that he had failed, that my value as secretary was more than the slim chance of my transformation to invisible superman. I spent the years in careful study, learning to read and write and count properly so that I could record my own data for him. I continued to distress his visitors, and memorized his intricate web of transactions so that I could advise him and remind him. He placed visitors with their back to my cage, and we devised a simple system of signs that I could give surreptitiously, behind their backs. At times they gave themselves away to me with a mumble while he posed against the far window.

I planned my replacement for him. He had started his experiments with the young, more an artistic choice than a scientific one. I argued that the subject needed much more complex, more experienced material, in order to transform. He had his doubts, but once Nerk was installed in my place, he nodded grudgingly.

"I never chose you, boy," the old man cried. "Don't do this. Don't you think I paid the price for you in my heart, all the time you've been in here? And the girl before you? And the others?"

"What was her name, Nerk?" I asked.

Turning my head, I said, "You see, master, there's an emotional component from which a younger subject simply does not benefit."

"I don't know, boy, any more than I know yours. There are so many… And I'm an old man. But I cared. I really cared." Nerk's eyes were hopeless, and I turned my back.

The master nodded. "There's something in what you say. When you came in, you didn't show the same sense of betrayal, quite."

"A child knows little of such things. It takes age to experience betrayal fully."

At our backs, Nerk subsided into a tangle of bones and belly as we retreated to the relative silence of the window.

"You may be right. I grant you that it generates more pressure, and pressure is what's needed, if my hypothesis is correct."

"Of course it is, master. But now we must focus on expanding the salt markets to the south-east." We turned to other matters.

Once I was out of the salt, it took little enough time to do my task. I took on more and more of the trivial, ministerial chores, and the correspondence, and finally the meetings themselves.

Now, he smiles up at me as the work goes on around us.

"I should have seen this coming," he admits.

I nod. "You neglected the effect of diffraction. At the proper angle, a thing can be seen even around a corner."

He cocks his head to one side. "Interesting indeed. But what effect would it have on my theory of transformation, do you think?"

I smile. "We shall see, master. We shall see." I step back to allow the workmen to set another block between us. "I've taken the liberty of increasing the pressure to account for it." On the floor below us, workmen remove the salt piping that ran through the master's bedroom, and they spray the new plug with brine that will crystallize in the interstices and act as mortar. "I expect careful records, mind."

"Of course." They seal the final block in place, leaving us to ourselves.

After a time, the visitors that do enter the House are again disappointed. The salt room has become repellent, I fear. The master has not maintained his focus on cleanliness, and he weeps dreadfully much of the time. I have faith, though, that he will transcend, that someday I will wake and look through my ceiling to find him gone. In her box beside my bed, Rula waits patiently to celebrate.

B. Morris Allen is a biochemist turned activist turned lawyer turned foreign aid consultant, and frequently wonders whether it's time for a new career. He's been traveling since birth, and has lived on five of seven continents, but the best place he's found is the Oregon coast. When he can, he makes his home there. In between journeys, works on his own speculative stories of love and disaster. His dark fantasy novel Susurrus came out in 2017.

The Sword of the Mongoose

By JIM BREYFOGLE

When a shady merchant loses a bet with Mangos, he has nothing to pay with but the story of where a masterwork blade may be found! Can Mangos reach his prize before other treasure hunters? All is not as it seems with this sought-after sword!

Six months after the fall of Alness.

Mangos moved his Mage forward. "The black Monarch has been defeated." He leaned back and grinned. "That's everybody, gentlemen. Pay up." He enjoyed the disgruntled muttering and the chink of silver from the losers.

He swept four small piles of coins into his pouch. It was good to win. Regum had *style*, sophistication. He winked at his partner, Kat, sure she would be impressed, before turning to the fifth player.

"I, ah," the merchant licked his lips, his eyes darted around the common room, obviously aware of everybody's interest, before settling back on Mangos, "don't have the money."

An appreciative murmur seemed to curl through the room like smoke from the fire. Men looked up from their ales, some nudged neighbors who hadn't heard. Regum was an entertaining game, but it became better when it led to a blood feud. The immediate consensus was that Mangos could crush the welshing merchant, but opinion was divided on whether he could get the value of the bet.

"You must have been sure you'd win," Kat purred as she circled the table, drawing the merchant's gaze until his head turned so far he had to snap it back the other way like an owl. But in this case he looked more like a mouse than an owl.

"My debt's not to you," the merchant said. "*You* didn't even play."

"*I* did," Mangos said, nodding to the Regum board. "And I won." It surprised him this scrawny little man would risk cheating. "Do you have silver teeth? I can take those." By custom, he was within his rights to kill the man.

The merchant licked his lips. "Better. I didn't want to do this, but I'll pay you with a story. A story and a Marin sword."

Mangos narrowed his eyes. "Stories don't buy ale." But a Marin sword... that was something else altogether.

"Listen and decide." The merchant's eyes

79

flickered around. Kat stood between him and the door. "Let me tell you of a man in trouble," he began, and the crowd leaned forward to hear his words.

"And so," he concluded a few minutes later, "the Earl of Riverside decided to hide his sword so the Priests of An Lorum couldn't demand it as his penance."

"As tales go, that's not a very good one," Mangos said.

"Just before crossing into An Lorum, he found a rock overlooking the river—"

"Stop!" Mangos said, slapping his palm on the table, making the coins and Regum pieces jump. He glared around the common room. All the other men hastily looked away, but Mangos wasn't fooled. "The story I will share, the sword I will not. Its location is for me alone!"

The merchant nodded. "Very well." He leaned forward and began to whisper in Mangos's ear, all about markers, locations, and keys.

"Why should we believe you?" Kat said bluntly.

"Here," the merchant passed Mangos a small bronze coin. "A *noblis* of Riverside. Not worth five silvers, but a token of my veracity." He glanced at the Regum board and sighed. "I had thought it would bring me luck."

Kat snorted. "It proves nothing."

The merchant spread his hands, palms up. He raised his voice, "Is there a soothsayer here?"

A young man cleared his throat. "I have a touch of the sight." His friends pushed

him forward, no doubt hoping to know the truth as well.

The merchant spoke slowly and clearly. "After making myself familiar with the details in the story, I believe there to be a sword hidden where I described, and that it surely is a Marin blade."

Mangos looked at the soothsayer. "He is telling the truth," the young man said.

"You believe him?" Kat demanded as the tavern door slammed behind the merchant. She curled her lip, making her opinion clear.

"It's not impossible, and you heard the soothsayer," Mangos said. He idly played with the bronze *noblis* as he thought of the merchant's story. The Earl of Riverside had died in the Priests' dungeon where he scratched his secret on the wall.

"It's not likely," Kat said, still standing. "He writes in code, and a hundred years later *this* merchant buys the information from another prisoner who broke the code?"

"Still," Mangos said, "a Marin sword. Do you have any idea what one is worth?"

"More than a five-silver tavern bet," Kat retorted.

"I could have killed him," Mangos said, tapping a coin on the tabletop. "It's worth his life."

"You still can kill him. If you want to go after the sword, you should catch him to keep as guide and hostage."

"Either the sword is there or it isn't," Mangos said. "Unless I want to kill him if it isn't, it makes no sense to take him hostage." He saw Kat's expression and laughed. "Isn't the lure of adventure worth five silvers? Besides, I have no wish to be knifed as I sleep.

"Marin made the first silvecite-alloyed swords," Mangos continued. How could he explain what that meant to a collector? He prided himself on knowing his steel. "Not only are Marin swords strong, well edged, and perfectly balanced, they're works of art."

"Which means you won't find them hidden alongside the road."

Mangos shook his head slowly. Owning a Marin sword would mark him as a dangerous man, a man of success and refinement. It was everything he wanted when they went to Alomar, for it would smooth his way in the city. "It doesn't hurt to check," he mused.

Kat snorted and flipped her hair back as if to say, *It's your call.* "The soothsayer did verify his words." She contemplated the Regum board. "He must have really believed he could win."

Mangos laughed. "But he didn't, and now I have his secret."

Kat lowered her voice. "The others heard the tale, and that the sword lies under a rock just this side of An Lorum. That's a very small area to look."

Mangos stood up. Only he knew the markers, but Kat was right, it was a small enough area that others would try their luck. "Let's hurry," he said.

"I'd expect a dozen men, plus whatever friends and cousins they can enlist," Mangos said. He could see two ahead of them, local youths of the sort who might go off adventuring to avoid farm work. They started to run when they saw Mangos and Kat. He wasn't worried. The boys couldn't run for three days.

He knew of others behind, men who hung back but would pass them at first opportunity. Pass them, or, when the stakes were as high as a Marin sword, kill them.

"Shall we step up the pace?" Kat asked, her tone light.

To answer, Mangos lengthened his stride. They started to gain on the boys who, when they noticed, began to run again. It became almost a game. The boys would run until they tired, then Mangos and Kat would close the gap, and the boys would run again. Each run was shorter, each time the gap closed more until Mangos and Kat passed them. The boys, red-faced and panting, shook their heads and turned for home.

"The others won't give up so easily," Kat said.

They might not, Mangos thought, but he was confident once he had a Marin sword he could best any living man.

The land rolled ahead of them, green grass cropped short by sheep and spotted with grey boulders. There were few trees and they could see for miles.

The sun outstripped them and retired for the night, but they kept moving by moonlight. Only when the moon set did they take shelter behind a large rock.

Early morning light woke Mangos. Some silent sense made him nervous, and he nudged Kat awake with his foot. Her eyes flew open, and she sat up and looked around.

A hawk cried.

"Just a hawk," Mangos said, feeling relieved.

"A white merlin? That's a noble bird. It doesn't belong to some local youth. Somebody else has gotten word of your Marin sword. I'd guess they're late to the chase, but probably mounted."

"That's *my* sword," Mangos said with righteous indignation. "I won the Regum game."

Kat didn't answer. Mangos dug in his pack for food as they started walking again.

The white merlin disappeared, but hours later it was back, circling. Kat stopped, breathing heavily, and looked back. "Look behind us."

A man and his dog stalked them several miles back, a couple miles behind him a group of four men walked, and another three beyond them. But far, far back, just visible at the top of the furthest ridge, rode a dozen horsemen.

The group of three had disappeared, and the four fallen further back. The man and his dog were now two valleys back, but the horsemen were only three ridges back, and Mangos was tired. He leaned over, hands on his knees as he tried to catch his breath.

"We're going to have to rest," he said. Kat nodded, too winded to speak.

Clouds were gathering and he wondered where they came from. He had not noticed them blowing in. In spite of his words, he started down into the next valley, pushed

by the images of the horsemen.

Another road ran along the valley floor and intersected their road. A wagon sat at the crossroads. The horse, a dun mare, drank at a stone trough while a man rubbed it down. Battered pots and worn tools hung from the wagon's sides. Mangos could see other goods, all used, inside the canvas cover.

When the man saw them he dropped his rag and drew a curved sword. He called to somebody out of sight and a woman's voice answered.

"She's Alnessi," murmured Kat as she glanced up at the clouds and raised her hood.

Refugees. The fall of Alness had scattered her citizens across the world. That was why they were selling junk. Likely they scavenged their goods as they fled their country.

"Merchants," Mangos said as a man moved between them and the wagon.

"Barely merchants," Kat said, "and they're worried about us being bandits."

"We've nothing you want," called out the man, his voice accented.

That's pretty clear, Mangos thought. "We weren't planning on taking any of it." *How do they sell anything if they don't have anything people want?*

Kat turned so she faced Mangos but had her back to the others. "He's Hafizi," she murmured, but Mangos didn't know who the Hafizi were or why one would be travelling with an Alnessi merchant. "Dangerous."

"Wait," Mangos said. "Maybe we do want something. Which way are you going?"

"South," said a woman, stepping out from behind the wagon. She was barely a woman, a girl really, and looked thin and worn.

"We'll pay you to take us west," Mangos said.

"No," the man said.

"Celzez," the woman said with a wave for him to keep quiet. "How far, and how much?"

"Twenty, twenty-five miles," Mangos said. "We'll pay five silvers." There was a certain symmetry in five silvers, the value of the tale.

"Take us two days out of our way for five silvers?" The girl snorted.

"One day," Mangos protested.

"Two, we have to come back."

Overhead, the merlin cried.

"Ten silvers," Mangos shrugged.

"Twenty."

A few heavy drop of rain fell, raising puffs of dust on the road. Mangos glanced behind them. "But we travel quickly, no lagging."

The girl nodded. "I'm Jalani. This is Celzez. Climb on."

Mangos settled in the back, trying to find space among the junk. The wagon might travel slowly, but at least they could rest as it moved.

"You're Alnessi?" Mangos asked, more to fill the silence than anything else.

"I am," Jalani said. "Celzez was my father's Hafizi guard. My father was a merchant." She said the last with a note of defiance.

"You're a long way from Alness."

"Celzez saved me from the fighting, and we escaped the city," Jalani said. "We found this wagon. I suppose we stole it, though the owners were dead. The best we could do was bury them."

She snapped the reins.

"We caught the horse running wild, no idea who owned it, gathered such goods as hadn't been broken or burned and headed south. We've been living as tinkers and petty merchants ever since."

Looking around the sorry merchandise, Jalani shook her head. "A poor start to rebuilding my father's business."

Nodding absently, Mangos stared out the back. He laughed to see the first men start to run when they saw the wagon. They might gain for a bit, but the last two days travel had been brutal, they had to be as exhausted as he was. They could never keep the pace.

But further back, dust rose from the hooves of a dozen horses. They could not outrun this pursuit; they could only hope to reach the sword's hiding place first.

"That hill there," Mangos said, pointing to a low hill rising up from the valley floor below them. The rain had grown heavier the closer they came to the valley, and now it fell like a lace curtain, making everything grey and hazy.

A river meandered along the broad valley floor, passing on the far side of the hill. Dead trees dotted its banks.

A bridge, long, old, and solid, spanned the river, the top of its arch visible above the hill. Just upstream a tower perched on a rocky island; the flood line of discolored stone was higher than the first floor.

Mangos studied the bridge and tower. "No doubt at all." He turned his attention back to the hill, searching for signs of the sword's hiding place.

"They're close," Kat said, pointing to the horsemen behind.

"Faster!" Mangos urged Jalani.

"No faster," Jalani answered. "Speed downhill will ruin a horse."

Mangos jumped from the wagon. "We can go faster on foot." He began to run.

"Hey!" shouted Jalani. "You still have to pay us!"

"Meet us on that small hill!" Mangos shouted back. He slipped in the mud but kept running.

At the top of the hill, Kat looked around. "You said there should be a marker stone…" She trailed away as she searched the tall grass and short bushes along the side of the road.

The tower stood closer now, three levels of dark stone with slate shutters and roof. The shutters of the first level were closed, but an unnatural glow came from the open windows of the top floor.

The rain had found the seam between Mangos's hood and his cape. He could feel the wetness seeping down his back. Mangos shuddered, not sure if it were the blue glow or the cold rain that sent shivers down his spine. He reminded himself that a Marin sword equaled respect. By owning one he would command better jobs and higher pay. The drinks and pleasurable company would

come easy. *Alomar will swoon at my feet,* he thought.

"Over here," Kat called.

Mangos hurried over. Wet grass obscured the overturned road marker. "Now to find the first stone. Ten paces east," he said, starting to walk the distance, "two paces south." He stopped beside a large stone. "Roll the stone." He dried his hands on the front of his tunic where it was still dry and took a grip on the stone. With a heave, he rolled it over.

There was a small cavity underneath with a largish piece of stone inside. At first glance it looked like whatever was hidden there had been taken and the side collapsed, but Mangos knew he needed the stone. He picked it up and grinned at Kat. "Just like we were told."

Kat nodded. "Hurry."

The horsemen were halfway down the valley—close enough to see the riders' armor and weapons.

Mangos carried the stone to the other side of the road, closer to where the tower brooded over the river, the blue light even more ominous in the heavy rain.

"It should be over here somewhere," he said, looking over the stones on the top of the hill. He paced around one, examining it from every side.

"It can't be this easy," Kat said.

Mangos pushed the stone. It wouldn't move. He moved to another spot and took a better grip. He couldn't budge the stone. "I *should* be able to move that," he said. He brushed some water from a small depression, an action that had no discernable effect.

He set the stone from under the first rock on the second stone, wiggling it until it settled snugly into the depression. He couldn't repress a grin.

The stone rolled easily with his next effort. He held his breath as a cavity came into view.

There *was* a sword.

And it was beautiful. The blade was straight and true, without the least sign of rust. The guard was skillfully fashioned to look spare and elegant but still protect his hand. The pommel looked to be a work of art. He reached down to pick up the sword and examined it more closely.

"It looks like a Marin sword," he breathed as he lifted the sword from the ground.

A thunderous crack exploded overhead, and the sky opened up. Rain fell in torrents, so hard it weighed on his head and shoulders. He couldn't see the bridge, the tower, or the wagon. He could barely see Kat standing beside him.

Nonetheless he swung the sword, cutting through the rain and marveling at its balance. He squinted at the pommel and ran his hand along the flat of the blade.

"It's real!" he exulted. "A true Marin blade!"

Wealth, respect, power—Mangos held it all in his hand. Even in corrupt Alomar, a Marin sword would turn heads.

"Too easy," Kat muttered. She paced away but returned to look at the sword. "Still too easy." She shook her head.

Mangos laughed and swung the sword again.

The rain slackened.

Kat froze. "You'll want to look at this."

Mangos lowered the sword and followed her gaze. The river had jumped its banks and was flooding around the approach to the bridge. It rose as he watched, climbing further. The rain dripping down his back felt unusually cold. "That's not natural," he said.

The water already rushed over the roadway. The dead trees stuck from the water like claws with white ribbon cuffs of whitewater trailing downstream.

Mangos shuddered at the mere thought of swimming that flood. "We can't go that way."

"Or back."

Mangos turned. The flood had flanked the hill and was rioting across the valley, turning the boulder-strewn ground into a treacherous mass of swirling white water.

Caught at the far edge of the flood, the horsemen scrambled back up the valley side. On the near side, Jalani and Celzez coaxed and prodded their tired horse to climb faster.

As one, Mangos and Kat turned to look at the tower. The blue light pierced the still heavy rain.

"I'd like to be a little further away from that," Mangos said.

"Cut the horse free!" Kat yelled to Jalani. The flood already lapped at the wagon's back wheels.

Jalani shook her head, but Celzez drew his curved sword and cut the traces. The wagon rolled back and freed the horse from the shafts. The flood lifted the back end of the wagon and pulled it completely into the water. It turned as it moved downstream, briefly hanging up on a tree before breaking free and rushing away.

"So," said Celzez. "We are here. Are we to just wait to drown?"

Mangos turned completely around. It seemed likely. The water raged over the abutments of the bridge, it swirled above the door on the tower, and it climbed the slopes of the hill where he stood.

"What's that?" He pointed to the tower where something moved.

The door opened, a glowing portal under the flood.

"Magic," hissed Jalani.

The water before them swirled. A hole opened in the center, and the water spun outward, revealing a tunnel stretching out toward the tower.

Far down the tunnel, shadows moved, shuffling forward to resolve into the forms of men.

The men's faces were pale and waxy, blemished by scrapes, bites, and gouges. Black and bloated hands hung like blood sausages from the ends of their arms.

Kat hissed, a sound of surprise and revulsion. "Revenants!"

Undead servants of a necromancer. Mangos felt a chill in his guts.

A dozen revenants issued from the tunnel and circled the hill. Their complete indifference to the rain, the mud, and anything the living could do, was harrowing. The final revenant, a man who must have been a smith in life, judging from his leather trou-

sers and apron, lifted a black hand and pointed to the tunnel.

The merchant gulped. "Maybe the necromancer is offering us sanctuary."

"That's a sanctuary I don't want to take," Kat said.

"We may not have a choice," Mangos replied.

Jalani jerked her head up and down, sending drops of water flying. "I think we should risk it. The upper levels of that tower should be safe."

"Not safe," Mangos and Kat said at the same time.

The revenants took a step forward, and the dead smith pointed again.

"Celzez?" Jalani asked.

"We should not go down that tunnel," Celzez said. He swung his sword through the rain. "We should kill them here."

"They're already dead," Jalani said. Her voice cracked as the revenants took another step closer.

Mangos stabbed the one nearest him. His Marin sword slid in easily, a blow that would have killed a man. The revenant pawed at the sword like it wanted to push it away.

"Don't make them angry!" the merchant moaned.

The revenants took another step, and the smell of rot and mold washed over them. With a whimper, Jalani broke away and slipped and slithered through the mud to the tunnel.

"Jalani!" called Celzez. "Jalani!" He hurried after her.

"Damn," muttered Kat.

"It's Hell and high water here," Mangos said. He jerked his sword free. "Maybe the Necromancer does offer safety," he said, though he didn't believe it.

"No. He doesn't. They never do." Kat twisted away from a revenant as it stepped forward, but there was another beside it. They stood shoulder to shoulder, two deep in places, and behind them the water still rose.

"Let's go," Mangos said. "Even if we could kill them, we can't escape the flood."

It was like stepping inside a waterspout laid on its side. Water twisted around them, it sounded angry. Only an inch of sorcery held back death, and Mangos had little faith in it.

They went single file, for only a narrow strip of ground showed at the bottom, and nobody seemed inclined to step on the curved water walls that somehow circled the tunnel in spite of intersecting the ground. The revenants clustered behind them, expressionless, crowding them forward.

"Necromancers," Mangos muttered, aware of the stink, but not knowing if it came from the revenants or the river muck. "He's not making a good impression."

"They never do," Kat said. "They live on the borders, just close enough to grab people to use in their magic but far enough away to avoid important people's wrath."

Jalani and Celzez hesitated to climb out of the riverbed to the glowing door, but the revenants kept coming, dragging their feet through the mud and puddles. Even worse, the far end of the tunnel had collapsed and

brown, frothing water followed the revenants toward them. "We can't stay here," Mangos said.

Celzez lifted Jalani up the riverbank. Kat followed. Mangos gave the revenants and the shortening tunnel one last look before climbing up and entering the necromancer's tower.

The door slammed shut, and water boomed against it as the tunnel completely collapsed. Water trickled around the frame, darkening the wood.

Silence, then the plink of water dripped from the rocks. The room was empty except for a set of stairs coiling up the far side of the tower to the next floor.

The revenants leaned against the outer wall and slumped, all semblance of life leaving them. Now they were just corpses piled against the walls, flaccid and motionless, all staring eyes, slack jaws, and rivulets of dried blood.

"We're underwater," Jalani said, looking very young and very scared.

We were before, Mangos thought, but didn't say it.

The water plinked again.

Black iron lanterns held globes of blue light. It gave the others a pale, sickly hue. *No different than the revenants. Is this what we'll become?* he wondered.

"I, ah, don't much like it here," Jalani said.

"We'll like it less when it floods," Celzez said. He stomped his foot and water splashed.

"We'd best be moving up," Kat said. She

put action to her words, going over to the stairs.

Mangos gestured Jalani and Celzez forward. He followed them up, only stopping once to watch the water creeping over the corpses.

Kat was already prowling the second floor.

Shelves of bottles and boxes lined the tower. More bottles covered a table in the center of the room, and strings of dried…stuff—Mangos didn't know what it might be—hung from the ceiling. It still smelled of decay, but of spice and ash and something animal as well.

"Dragon's blood," Kat said as she studied the rows of bottles. "Tanis leaf. Heela spikes—that's impressive."

"You know these things?" Jalani asked.

Kat nodded. "Very rare, very dangerous, very expensive."

Jalani nodded, exhaustion etched on her face. She sank into a black chair half hidden by the table.

"Don't sit there!"

Jalani jumped up. Kat shook her head. "Arcane." She drew their attention to a large basin behind the chair with her sword point. "Quicksilver." She then pointed to a giant stone font. A wooden lid covered it. As she took the lid, she closed her eyes as if overcome with emotion. "Life," she said, "This is where the necromancer harvests his victims' lives to fuel his magic."

A warm yellow glow filled the room.

The lid slammed closed, seemingly by itself. Kat tried to open it again, but her hand slipped off.

"Do not touch what does not belong to you." A cloaked and hooded figure stood on the stairs to the third level.

"Then you shouldn't leave it out," Kat said. "It isn't really yours. It belongs to those downstairs."

"You criticize me? Do you not know who I am?" He lifted both hands to lower his hood. It was the story-telling merchant from the inn.

Mangos felt his jaw drop open and he closed it with a snap. "Damn you! This was all to trap us?"

"Not just you," the necromancer said. "That story was aimed at every adventurer in the room. But," he shrugged, "you carried the trigger for the flood."

Mangos thought of the bronze *noblis* he carried. Then another thought crossed his mind. "You owe me five silver pieces!"

"Fool!" roared the necromancer. "I am the right hand of Death himself."

Jalani let out a soft whimper. Celzez stood in front of her. His hand shook as he lifted his sword.

"I am the devourer of souls!" roared the necromancer.

It seemed the darkness in the nooks of the tower grew deeper.

"I am the render of the creation." The man's words shook the very air.

"You own the tower where I'll be staying until the waters recede," Mangos said.

"I am ISAK YAN!" the necromancer shouted. "The waters recede when I say they'll recede, and you'll be staying much longer than that."

"Will you be serving dinner?"

"I don't think," said the necromancer, "you appreciate what is about to become of your life."

I think I do, thought Mangos, feeling the ice in his stomach and what felt like spiders walking on the back of his neck. *But if he can try to scare us, I can laugh at him.* Yet while Mangos felt scared, the necromancer wasn't laughing.

Isak Yan pointed to Jalani. "You are about to replenish my cauldron. Sit." When Jalani didn't move he said, "All I need do is call the revenants."

Keeping one eye on Isak Yan, Mangos went to the stairs. Something moved in the blue water, shadows that resolved into men and began to climb toward the surface.

The first revenant rose up, water dripping. Mangos slashed, opening a large gash that did nothing to slow it. He kicked it back into the water, but two more replaced it. He had to retreat.

The revenants were stiff and awkward but deceptively fast. While two attacked Mangos, others rushed past.

Celzez defended Jalani while Kat carved the hands from a revenant threatening her.

Isak Yan stood above them, watching. He lifted a hand.

Mangos's vision swirled, and the world tilted. The ground wasn't where his feet were, or so it seemed, and he fell. Across the room he saw Celzez fall before revenant feet, black and scabby, blocked his vision.

He rolled and rose, lurching and flailing as the room swam. "Beware sorcery!" he shouted as swung, somehow separating a revenant's head from its neck.

Kat dropped her sword and grabbed two large flasks from the table.

"No!" shouted Isak Yan. Mangos's balance returned as Isak Yan faced Kat and lifted his arms above his head. His hands sparkled as he thrust them toward Kat. Kat smashed one flask before the sparks enveloped her like a swarm of fireflies. The little, twinkling lights settled on her and she slowed and stopped moving, the second flask tilted and her free hand reaching for her dagger.

Isak Yan lifted his sleeve to mop his face.

A sharp scream pierced the air. Jalani struggled in the grip of a revenant while Celzez tried futilely to reach her.

"Give up," Isak Yan said.

"Not likely." Nearly surrounded, Mangos could only put the stairwell at his back and try to keep the revenants from grappling him.

Cold hands grabbed his wrists. A revenant climbing from below pulled his arms back. He felt cold, wet flesh pressing against his back, and the stench of rot filled his nostrils. He struggled, but the hands pinching his wrists, hard bone gripping through flaccid muscles, held him tight.

"You see how fruitless your struggle is?" Isak Yan said.

Mangos kicked backwards, hoping to catch the revenant holding him by surprise. He struck hard, but with no result.

"It doesn't seem you do. You'd better bring me his sword." Isak Yan gestured and a revenant tore the sword from Mangos's grip.

"Give it back!" Mangos shouted, renewing his struggle. The Marin blade was irreplaceable!

Isak Yan came down and took the blade. He turned it over and held it up to the light. "Very, very nice. You are, indeed, a man of taste and accomplishment," he mocked. He laid it on the table. "It shall go back in the ground for the next adventurer to find."

"Fool to bury it!" Mangos snarled. He needed a sword; he wanted that one.

Isak Yan shrugged. "Telling the truth helps lure otherwise suspicious folk."

Mangos lunged forward, but again could not break free. He could not expect help, either. Kat strained against the magic holding her, but couldn't do more than quiver. Four revenants hemmed in Celzez, and Jalani could not break free of the revenant holding her.

"Bring me the girl," Isak Yan commanded.

The revenant dragged Jalani over to the ebony chair.

Isak Yan came down the stairs, extended his hands over the bowl of quicksilver, and began to murmur arcane words.

Mist gathered over the bowl, silver and faintly luminous. It grew thick and began to swirl, spinning into threads and from threads into ropes.

Jalani moaned as the ropes drifted to her, wrapping around her arms and legs, binding her to the chair. She closed her eyes and seemed to grow smaller as she shrank back.

Isak Yan drew a long, black knife. He reached into a dark corner and seemed to cut the air. He pulled back a piece of darkness and pulled it over Jalani's head.

A hood of shadows, Mangos thought.

Celzez roared, bashing aside the revenants in front of him and rushing at Isak Yan. He raised his curved sword as he attacked.

Isak Yan lifted his other hand. "You...can't...win," he said, his teeth clenched and muscles tight.

Celzez slowed, as if he pushed against greater and greater resistance. He started to swing his sword, but it moved with glacial slowness and finally stopped altogether.

Isak Yan quivered with the effort of all his magic.

Kat's hand shook. The liquid in the flask she held crept over the lip. A thick, syrupy fluid, it caught the light as it stretched, slowly, to the floor. Smoke twisted up as it touched the spilled contents of the flask she dropped earlier.

The two liquids exploded, lifting Kat from her feet and throwing her across the room. The blast cleared everything from the table. Heat washed across Mangos.

With a cry of exertion, Mangos flexed to free himself. The revenant clung to his wrists; he was pulling it more tightly against his back. With an awful tearing sound, he pulled free.

He had torn off the revenant's arms; they still clung to his wrists.

He started to use them to club the revenants around him.

"Kill the necromancer," Kat said. She climbed to her feet, clothes singed and a dazed expression on her face.

With these weapons? Mangos wondered. *At least I'm armed.*

He knocked the revenants back, but couldn't stop them. The Marin sword had been lost in the explosions, blown somewhere out of sight. Kat had taken Celzez's sword and cut the head from a revenant, but she was barely holding back several others.

"I don't want them to kill you," Isak Yan said.

He just wants to kill us himself. Mangos needed to attack the necromancer directly, for the revenants would eventually win. He could not outlast the undead.

He avoided the blundering charge of an armless revenant. *Madness*, he thought. His eye settled on a sword hilt amongst the mess on the floor—his Marin blade.

Mangos dove forward and grabbed the sword; it settled into his hand, feeling like an extension of his arm. It was perfectly balanced, perfectly proportioned. *A man could do amazing things with this*, he thought.

Mangos uncoiled in a lunge, stretching as far as he could, and was rewarded by striking Isak Yan. Isak Yan parried too late, swiping after the sword had sunk deep into his chest.

The black knife cracked against the Marin blade. The knife dissolved into shadows that disappeared in the corners of the room. The Marin blade vibrated, letting off a low moan before it shattered.

Isak Yan gasped, and all motion stopped.

The revenants collapsed, the quicksilver ropes binding Jalani splashed to the floor, and the hood of shadows disappeared.

Isak Yan hunched over, clutching at his chest as if he could draw out the portion of blade still inside him. He dropped to his knees and collapsed completely.

"He broke my sword," Mangos said, staring at the hilt in disbelief.

Kat nodded. She went over to the window and opened the shutter a crack.

"He broke my sword," Mangos repeated.

"I heard you." Kat opened the shutter wide. "It stopped raining."

"That sword was worth a fortune."

Jalani blinked in the light. She seemed dazed. "You saved my life."

"But you cost her the wagon and all her trade goods," Celzez said.

"I lost my sword," Mangos said.

Kat stared at both of them and started to prowl the room. "Sell this," she told Jalani. "Instead of that junk you had, sell all of this." She stopped by the font. "Even the life essence."

Celzez protested, "We only want the value of what we lost. This is worth much, much more."

A small smile stole over Kat's lips, "Are you on her side or not? We're adventurers, not merchants; and you fought the battle too."

Their conversation barely registered with Mangos as he gathered the shards of his Marin blade. He cupped them carefully in his hands, thinking how few they seemed. He took them to the window and threw them into the receding flood.

Jim Breyfogle currently resides in Pennsylvania. When he isn't writing he is gathering an army of terracotta warriors with which to aggravate his English Mastiff—thus far, the dog still wins.

When Gods Fall in Fire

By BRIAN K. LOWE

Compelled by magic to serve his master Duke Ciero, Lairc has brought the grasping nobleman to his long-sought prize! But at what price comes the limitless power offered by Amad-ad-Yomat, the strange divinity that fell from the stars!?

Lairc halted in the doorway of the deserted house, sniffing the air, unconsciously bringing his sword into a guard position.

"What's wrong? Keep moving!" hissed the man behind him.

"There's magic here."

"Of course there is! That damned priest promised me you would be able to sense it." Ciero, the Grey Duke, shoved hard. "He *also* promised me your obedience. Go in there."

Lairc entered the room stiffly and in halting steps. He listened carefully before sheathing his sword and bringing out flint and fuel to examine the room by the flickering light. Anything of value was long gone. He even looked at the ceiling, but saw only time-worn wood.

"I see nothing... your grace."

Duke Ciero huffed, and as he entered, something scuttled along the wall over his head, something that had not been there before. It dropped toward the unsuspecting duke even as Lairc whipped out his blade and drove it home. Ciero hadn't time to duck.

"Are you mad?" the duke demanded.

Lairc pulled his sword free, holding it so Ciero could see the fist-sized, yellow-striped blob impaled there.

"It's a tiger spider. Someone put it under a veil. Remember I said I smelled magic in the doorway? I used to smell the same smoke when they crafted veils in the marketplace in Xhousun."

"Set it on the *second* man to walk into the room... Clever." Ciero's eyes narrowed. "You could have let it kill me."

"I could. But then I would have been trapped in here with it."

The duke leaned forward, his gloved finger extended. He touched the tiny thing and jerked back as if bitten. The fingertip of his glove was smoking.

"The tiger spider is very venomous, your grace," Lairc murmured. "Perhaps you shouldn't touch it."

"You could've warned me!"

Lairc smiled thinly. Ciero carefully removed the glove, threw it into a corner, and backhanded Lairc across the face.

Wearing his new welt like a badge, Lairc crossed to where the discarded glove had fallen, carefully using it to scrape the spider and its venom off his blade. He remained on one knee and felt about.

"There is a trap door here, your grace."

"I was told there would be." The duke gestured impatiently. "Raise the door."

Lairc did so, then carefully descended into the ground, a descent marked not by increasing darkness, but light.

Not waiting for his master, he moved down the short tunnel until he heard men's raised voices. He stopped in the shadows to listen. Two men, lean and muscular, shared their coloring and bone structure with a third man, who was entering a well-fed middle age.

"It's hot in this damned hole," said one of the younger men.

"Believe me, Artus, it's hotter in hell, and that's where we'll be if the king finds us."

"Yes, Artus, stop whining," pleaded the oldest. "I'll see to it you get the royal villa in the Casares if you just stop whining about the heat. Nice ocean breezes."

"*You'll* see to it, Gruntal? Who died and made you king?"

"An interesting question," interposed the duke, stepping into view. "A pity you won't hear the answer."

The three turned slowly.

"Your grace," purred the eldest. He slid his sword free, and the others mirrored him. "Judging from your retinue, I take it you are here on your own behalf."

"You can't take us, Ciero," Artus said. "You couldn't take any of us, let alone all three." He motioned with his chin to Lairc, who had not drawn his weapon. "What's he—"

Artus fell where he stood, his last words hanging on the air, the duke's man in a guard position over his body, the blood spray barely dripping. Gruntal and his brother jumped back in shock.

"A pity," the duke said in a voice that belied his words. "I might have let you live if you'd just given me the map. I could have used your experience in my government. But now..." He glanced down at Artus's body. "Your brother was a fool. Lairc was a gladiator slave in Khure."

Gruntal's eyes narrowed. "You're lying. There's no such thing."

Ciero shrugged.

"Lairc, is it?" Gruntal said, his sword tip wavering between the two men before him. "Whatever Ciero's paying you, we can double it. All you have to do is kill him, and everything else is forgotten."

Lairc's eyes glittered.

Ciero sniffed. "Your loyalty to your late brother is touching, but it won't help. Lairc had a geas placed on him by his former master. I'm sure he would like nothing better than to run me through, but he can't."

The brothers exchanged a glance and committed their last mistake. One leaped at Lairc, the other for the duke. They died within heartbeats of each other without Ciero ever drawing steel.

"I hope you didn't get blood on the map."

Lairc wiped his sword on Gruntal's cloak before sheathing it, then searched the body. He held out what he had found to the duke.

"There *is* blood on it, your grace. I... apologize."

"Find something to wipe it off, you fool."

Lairc wiped the map on Ciero's shirt.

"I'll make sure the way is clear, your grace," he said and turned toward the tunnel.

"You know, much as I disliked them, any one of those men would have made a better king than I will. And yet you killed them for me. What do you think of that?"

"I think it makes them luckier than me," Lairc replied. "At least they died free."

The sun was a bloody eye sinking toward an impaling peak, black the shadow that reached almost to the hooves of the horses. Already the cool of the coming night was biting through Ciero and Lairc's clothing. They had already endured three of these cold nights.

Just before sunset, they entered a narrow canyon, bare of any plant or animal life—or any exit.

"The trail leads through here," the duke announced, consulting the map. "We'll camp tonight and continue tomorrow."

"How can you read that thing?" Lairc's manner had deteriorated as the temperature fell.

Duke Ciero took his time folding the map.

"It's a map. I don't need to *read* it. When it says you cross a mountain, you cross a mountain. When it says to go through a canyon, you go through the canyon." He pointed slightly to their right. "It says go there, so that's what we'll do."

"But there's nothing there. We've been riding for days, and there's nothing there." Lairc's breathing grew ragged and his hand gripped the air near the hilt of his sword, but then a cloud passed over his face, and he relaxed. "As you say, my lord."

"Aye, as I say." Ciero shifted his position on the hard dirt. "Have you ever heard of the ancient city of Galtoun?"

"The Khureans don't teach history to their slaves. Not even Khurean history."

Ciero snorted without humor. "I doubt you'd want to know." He sighed. "Galtoun was supposed to have been built in a valley in these mountains hundreds of years ago. Some of the histories say the Galtouni were sorcerers—"

"Like the Khureans."

"Yes... I suppose so," Ciero responded. "Then one night a god fell on Galtoun and destroyed it in a flash of fire that filled the entire valley."

"A god?" Lairc shook his head. "A rock slide, more likely."

"Apparently not," the duke said. "For over a hundred years, men have died for this map. Something extraordinary fell on Galtoun, and the man who can retrieve it will be blessed beyond his wildest dreams."

"And you think this thing, this god, can make you king of Yanustan."

"I'm gambling my life that it can. And yours."

They began the next day stiff and surly, the cold retreating only reluctantly from the shadows.

The duke urged his horse forward at a walk toward a sheer cliff. When they had walked a hundred extra paces past the point where the visible path ended, they turned a corner and saw a channel between two rock walls.

"Someone didn't want this path discovered so easily," Ciero noted. "It almost took an act of faith."

"Then it was good there were two of us," Lairc said. "Because that means I wouldn't have found it."

The walls threatened every moment to close in, to block all forward progress. The stone scraped elbows and shoulders and bare flanks, making men and horses irritable and nervous. The walls fused overhead in places, robbing them of what little sun they had.

Soon, though, a line of light showing the end of the cleft appeared. When finally they emerged, the walls opening to admit the sun and present a low, wide valley, they halted in awe.

In the distance, graceful white towers rose to the clouds behind walls built for beauty, not for defense. Cultivated fields and orchards featured straight rows of fruit-laden trees and bushy plants. Men and women, some stripped to the waist, picked and pruned and hoed in the sun, and the sounds of song drifted their way faintly on the desultory breeze.

As they walked through the fields, men and women raised hands in greeting, smiling as they went back to work. Their clothes were stained and blotted with dirt and sweat, but it looked *good* on them, as medals earned.

"They seem glad to be working so hard," Ciero said.

Lairc's stride was looser than before, the tension of always watching his surroundings seeming to have deserted him.

"You've never known work. There's pride in a job well done."

"But it's dirty."

"And yet no one is making them do it."

"Don't get your hopes up," the duke said curtly. "No matter what the customs are like here, you're still bound to me."

They entered the temple's low-ceilinged courtyard through a wide entrance unencumbered by guards or attendants of any kind.

"It doesn't seem right," the duke said. "Usually temples are guarded, to keep out anyone who isn't planning to make a donation, and keep in the donations. And there aren't any moneylenders, or healers, or merchants…"

"They don't have any guards on the temples in Khure, either," Lairc said unexpectedly. "At least, not that you can see."

"Kind of like you," Ciero mused. "No bonds that you can see."

"The trouble with invisible chains, my lord, is that you can't tell when they've been broken."

The duke frowned, but his thoughts were interrupted by the arrival of a middle-aged bald man with a brown beard. He held his arms wide in welcome.

"My lord, worthy warrior, I am Brother Sion. Can I fetch some refreshments, or would you prefer to see the treasure of legend first?" Sion smiled impishly. Then he moved aside, indicating they should proceed. "You really should sit and take a drink. This is not going to be easy."

Ciero's face went slack with shock, but he allowed Sion to lead them to a set of low benches in a central atrium, where a man-servant appeared with water and a plate of fruits. Lairc unbuckled his belt and lay his sword on the ground. At a glance from Sion, Ciero belatedly did the same.

"The treasure you seek, your grace, is in this building." Sion pointed past Ciero's shoulder. "In there. Its name is Amad-ad-Yomat, and this is its temple."

Ciero's eyes narrowed as he leaned forward, then cast a glance back over his shoulder. Sion shook his head slightly.

"You can't see the god from here. You have to go to it—or I suppose I should say them. It doesn't matter; they don't get around much." He smiled at his own private joke. "A little more than one hundred years ago, Amad-ad-Yomat fell from the sky in a blazing fireball. They fell to earth on this spot, blasting a crater exactly the size of this building.

"It was harvest time, or else many would have been killed. As it was, we lost only a few. It took days for things to cool down enough for us to reach it. But even before that, we knew already Amad-ad-Yomat was not a simple fallen star."

"Wait," said the duke. "I thought you said this happened over a hundred years ago."

"He did, my lord," Lairc spoke up. "Pay attention. He said this was a god, after all."

Ciero shot him a look, but Sion went on despite the interruption.

"I am one hundred and thirteen years old, your grace. Amad-ad-Yomat barely survived its crash, and even now they are very fragile, but when they recovered their senses, they felt ashamed for the damage they had done, and taught us... well, to live to be one hundred and thirteen. And the building techniques that went into this temple, and agriculture, and science. Our children are all in school, learning things from Amad-ad-Yomat that our fossilized minds could never comprehend."

"Then the treasure of Galtoun is not riches, it is *power*."

"No, your grace, the treasure of Galtoun is *knowledge*. Knowledge that Amad-ad-Yomat is willing to share with us, in exchange for allowing them to live and grow here."

"Grow?" Lairc asked.

"Amad-ad-Yomat was badly injured in the crash. Many of them were killed. They are only now nearing their former numbers, and only then can they begin to repair their vessel. But they are still weak."

"You keep referring to it as 'they,'" the duke noted. "Why? Is there more than one Amad-ad-Yomat?"

"That is one of the concepts that the young accept better than we do." Sion shrugged. "Amad-ad-Yomat is—different from us. They come from a different place, a different world. I don't pretend to understand it, and they have made *me* their high priest. Sometimes I think it was just because I was the first to reach them."

"The ways of the gods are strange."

"Indeed, Lairc, they are." Suddenly Sion stood and clapped his hands. "It is time for our meal. The farmers will be coming in from the fields, and the workers returning home." The manservant reappeared.

"Mar'leh will show you to your rooms."

As they turned to leave, Sion called out. "My lord, Ciero. The temple is open all day and night. If you would like to come back later and make Amad-ad-Yomat's acquaintance, feel free." He smiled wryly. "And bring Lairc, if you wish."

"He knows why we're here." "Maybe he thinks the god can protect itself, your grace. There are only two of us. And why is that? If you really thought the treasure was enough gold and jewels to buy a kingdom, you'd have needed more men, or at least horses, to carry it. But here we are, just two men, no extra beasts, no servants..."

"It's none of your business what I expected to find."

"I think it's very much my business. Even a slave fights better when he knows why."

"Then the slave will have to fight blind. There may be a change of plans. Things are not as I had expected them. It makes me nervous."

"Really? Everyone here serves the same god, they work at the same time, they eat at the same time, they probably sleep at the same time. It seems normal to me."

Lairc played with the vegetables that seemed to form the main cuisine of Galtoun, pushing them around on his plate with a double-pronged eating tool.

Someone tapped on his door. Lairc looked up sharply.

"Enter."

In walked a woman with short blond hair and a long, slender frame.

"Good evening, Lairc. I'm Rina. I came to see that you were comfortable. Did you like your dinner?" Her voice was light, with a faint huskiness.

Lairc stood awkwardly. In his years in Khure, he had known his share of women, rewards for his skills—or nurses, sometimes, when his skill was lacking. But they had all been slaves themselves, with no more choice than he had... His breathing began to quicken.

She knelt and plucked a small yellow squash from his plate.

"Don't they eat vegetables where you come from?" she asked. "Let me show you the best way to dine in Galtoun." She dropped the squash back on his plate and touched her robe. "First you peel the outer layers away..."

After she had peeled away the outer layer, her student needed no further instruction.

Rina rose and began to dress. Lairc propped himself up on one elbow.

"Where are you going?"

She reattached the hidden catches that he would never have been able to find on his own, flashing him a small grin.

"I have to get back to my husband. He won't know how to make his own breakfast."

"You're *married?*"

"Oh, yes, four years now." She patted her stomach. "Amad-ad-Yomat says we are having a boy."

Lairc choked getting his words out. "But why? Why are you here if you're married? And with child?"

Rina leaned forward to kiss him. "Everyone does what he does best. Amad-ad-Yomat told me that, of all the women in Galtoun, I was the one whom you would want the most. I was quite honored." And with that she was gone.

In the morning, Sion took them to meet his god.

He met them in the courtyard where they had spoken the day before. Ciero was eager to start, Lairc less so. Sion responded to both the same.

"While we are walking, I would like to acquaint you with some of the things Amad-ad-Yomat has done for us. There are sights here you will see nowhere else in the world. Note these walls, for example."

"There are no corners," Lairc said.

"Yes," Sion responded, while the duke looked more closely as they passed. "Corners mark the boundary between rooms; here everything is part of one whole being."

"Like the people," Lairc murmured, causing the duke to turn an angry eye upon him.

"Quiet! Look around you. It's astounding."

"You all seem to be moving in the same direction," Lairc went on. "Toward the same goal."

Again Ciero shot him a daggered look, but Sion merely nodded.

"Amad-ad-Yomat was right about you, Lairc. They said that, freed from your geas, your natural intelligence would be impressive."

Ciero stared. "Free of his—do you mean that you've lifted his compulsion? The Khurean insisted it was the only way to control him! Do you have any idea what this man is capable of?"

They were passing through a large chamber with arched openings. Apart from a single tall vase set against one wall, it was empty.

"This room was designed by Amad-ad-Yomat for one purpose: to be admired. One may sit on this floor for hours, following the subtle geometries of the walls and ceiling. Note the smooth curve of the arches; they exist nowhere else."

The duke had moved several steps from his former slave, who ignored him.

"Did you hear what I said? He could kill us both before you could call for help."

"I know what Lairc is capable of, my lord duke...far better than you, in fact. It was why we had you bring him here."

"What are you talking about?"

Sion kept walking. "It will be easier to explain after you see Amad-ad-Yomat."

They entered a room whose end formed a large hearth with crackling logs the size of tables, before which stood an altar, flanked by two tall golden stands. Each held a small, bright flame that gave off almost no heat. The lamps were more impressive than the god, a pockmarked rock less than two hands across, sitting in a depression in the center of the altar. A golden railing circled the depression, and a protective lattice floated over the god's head like a halo.

Yet the presence that filled that room,

lighting the face of the high priest Sion with devotion, was nearly impossible to resist, and hopeless to deny.

"This is Amad-ad-Yomat, the god who fell in fire," Sion announced, his voice hushed. "They who summoned you here to take them out into the world."

And the Amad-ad-Yomat *spoke.*

We sailed ships of stone through endless seas against a backdrop of millions of stars and vast clouds of luminescent red and blue and yellow dust, thought alone filling our sails. Then disaster struck, and we fell to Earth from an incomprehensible height, barely surviving the explosive impact. With your help we can rise again to the heavens—and in our wake, the human race will follow.

"They want us to take them out of here," Ciero said slowly. "They will make me king."

"Yes, Ciero, they will make you king. We have done all that we can here. You will carry Amad-ad-Yomat away, with the mountain tribes falling in as an army behind you. Amad-ad-Yomat will teach you how to overcome your enemies, and their labors will make him stronger. And you, Lairc—Amad-ad-Yomat is still very weak. Its vessel could never stand the stresses of the void—nor even of the Earth. You will be the god's protector until they can rebuild their vessel. As king, Ciero can offer all of Yanustan's resources, but when even Yanustan is no longer enough, *you* will take them into the greater world. You will be their disciple, and kings will do your bidding."

Lairc stared at the rock as though he had heard none of Sion's words.

"Think of it, my friends. What Amad-ad-Yomat has done here, he can do for the whole world. There is no disease they cannot cure, no desert they cannot make bloom, no enemy they cannot bring to friendship. And all they ask in return is your help."

"That's all?" Lairc asked, his gaze locked on the stone. "Is it all they ask, that a woman with child should leave her husband to lie with another man? Is it all they ask that we should travel for days through bandit-haunted hills just so that we can be presented with their greatness?"

"You wanted to come here!" Sion protested. "You thought you would find gold or riches to buy your kingdom—and when Amad-ad-Yomat asked, Rina consented. There was no coercion. It was an honor to assist them—and you."

"An *honor?* There is no honor in slavery. No, nor choice either. I didn't want to come here—I was dragged here, whether by the duke or your god makes no difference."

"Lairc!" Ciero protested. "Amad-ad-Yomat can change the world. Whether slave or master, it matters not how you came here."

Lairc pushed his words past gritted teeth.

"It matters how *I* came here, *your grace.* I killed three men on your orders to be here, better men than you. But I was a slave then."

"Yes, you were a slave then. But Amad-ad-Yomat has set you free."

"Free? To serve it, to take it to and fro, so that other men may fight and die to do its bidding?"

Your Cover Your Way

DW Creations LLC
dwcreations.online

"For a price!" Sion insisted. "We have made a bargain, Lairc, and we will be paid handsomely!"

"Golden collars still make slaves!"

Before Sion could do more than choke out a protest, Lairc tore away the golden canopy, seized the rock with both hands, and raised it over his head.

"Lairc! Put that down!" Ciero shouted.

"Lairc, please," begged Sion. "You'll be like a king. Even the Khureans will bow before you."

"Even the Khureans?" Lairc hesitated. "Even the Khureans..."

And then he hurled the stone into the furnace behind the altar, where it cracked in half and fell into the flames.

The high priest dropped to his knees with a moan. Ciero stared open-mouthed at the empty altar and the furnace as if he could hear the dying god's screams.

Lairc was already at the doorway. "Are you coming, Ciero? I promise I won't kill you at least until we get out of the mountains."

"You've destroyed everything... I would have been king. And what about the townspeople?" the duke asked. "Their god is dead. What if the hillmen come down?"

"Then they'll get what their god couldn't give them. They'll die free."

Brian K. Lowe is a member of the Science Fiction and Fantasy Writers of America (SFWA), with over 40 story publications to his credit. His trilogy The Stolen Future, the fantastic adventures of a 20th century soldier stranded on a far-future Earth, was recently released by Digital Fiction Publishing. This is his fifth appearance in Cirsova.

My Name Is John Carter (Pt 7)

By JAMES HUTCHINGS

So we stumbled half-dead down a passage which led
to a metal-walled chamber within.
On a Spartan straw mat our deliverer sat
straight and tall, and sepulchrally thin.

He was shriveled and dry as a mummy that lies
under skies never sullied by cloud,
and his gaze seemed to hold all the secrets of old,
and his garb looked less garment than shroud.

Bowls of water, no more, were laid out on the floor,
but to us this seemed more than a feast,
so we wordlessly sank to our haunches and drank
as serene and as silent as beasts.

But by Nature's decree, we may not long be free
of that callous commander called Reason.
All too soon our content was as gold that is spent
and cold dread seized the reins from repletion.

For our savior and host had the look of a ghost
and the hairs on my neck would not settle
till our lucky escape took a sinister shape
and the room seemed a coffin of metal.

And a scream filled my mind--grew too urgent to
    bind--
then he spoke. And at once, all unease
was an error unlearned, was a shame to be spurned
was a mist blown away by a breeze.

For his voice was a song--as unstoppably strong
as the lust of a newlywed groom.

There was vigor inside that his body denied,
like a tiger that skulks in a tomb.

"Naught imperils thee here. Harken not to thy fear
which cries havoc at all that is strange.
By the ghost of the sea, thou art stranger than me,
yet I sit with composure unchanged."

"Well, I'm strangest," I smiled, "if you measure in
    miles,
but I'm damned if I see how you knew,
for that dyer the Sun makes all shades into one.
There's but little to mark me from you."

"Not by shade of your hide," the old Martian re-
    plied,
"but the shape of your lungs and your heart.
Matter lowers its shield, and all things are revealed
to the eyes that have mastered the art."

"Do not think yourself wise for the skill of your
    eyes."
Dejah Thoris looked up from her bowl.
"All the flesh may be shown and the man still un-
    known,
but the vision of love sees the soul."

For such love to be mine made the world seem to
    shine,
yet I felt even then that the glow
bore a cynical stain, like the scar stamped on Cain
or like blood on a pure field of snow.

101

MY NAME IS JOHN CARTER (PT 7)

For I knew very well that I never could tell
of the joy that suffused me in battle
when I no more felt pain for the men I had slain
than the slaughterman feels for the cattle.

If my lover were right, and true love could grant
    sight
of the soul, as the eyes see the face
'twould put end to all fear for the soul that was
    clear
and bring Hell to the soul that was base.

Then he spoke of much more; cities ancient before
the first gardens of Ur had been planted
and the secrets God wrote on the tiniest mote
and we questioned and listened, enchanted.

What is true? What is just? This and more we dis-
    cussed
till the last light of day had long fled.
Here was bounty indeed, and a new kind of greed
bid me gorge upon all that he said.

As we learned and debated the hour grew late
and he asked if I wanted to rest,
for my face had grown pale. Yet I felt whole and
    hale,
and a thirst to know more filled my breast.

But again I was wrong. I had fought for too long
and too long kept my terror in check
and too recently paced through a life-hating waste
and felt Death place his hands round my neck.

So I took little heed of my burgeoning need
till, inclined to dissent on some trifle,
I stood up and I cried that he shamefully lied
in a voice like the crack of a rifle.

Then he bade me forbear, and be silent, and stare
at a disk that he wore round his neck.
And I looked, and grew calm, and the sight seemed
    a balm

for the fear and fatigue of our trek.

There I saw every shade that the rainbow dis-
    played--
all and more: there were two other rays,
each an alien hue Earthly eyes never knew,
that entranced and tormented my gaze.

Once these colors (he said) were as common as red,
two more everyday gifts of the Sun.
They are gone with the rains, and a desert remains
and that glorious era is done.

Mars had paid a great cost when these colors were
    lost
for they held more than beauty alone.
One kept air in its place, that it not bleed to space.
By the other, the airships had flown.

Once the Sun freely gave—now the Martians must
    slave
and an order whose work never ceased
tended ancient machines by laborious means
with the zealous devotion of priests.

'Twas a millstone to grind any body and mind
and a burden that few folk could bear,
but their lives were well-spent, for naught else
    could prevent
a Barsoom that was stripped of all air.

If there's aught I detest, it is having to rest.
Sickness makes of the body a prison,
but the will may not choose to obey or refuse
battered flesh shrieking out its decision.

So I lay and I healed and the old man revealed
that a town called Zodanga lay near.
Dejah reckoned it wise that we went in disguise,
for the towns of the desert frontier

treat the precepts of law like the dry summer straw
that the smallest of sparks may consume

and who ventures to own they call Helium home
has called down inescapable doom.

The old man had a dye, and our skins were thereby
turned the shade of some race from afar
and, as Dejah's renown may have spread to the
town,
she was marked with a counterfeit scar.

This Zodanga, I thought, *is less township than fort.*
I had never seen walls reaching higher,
and a glowering guard stood on each lofty yard
with a rifle raised ready to fire.

As they stared from on high with an aquiline eye
and my knuckles grew white on my blade,
Dejah cried, in a tone that I thought overblown,
"We have come to thy city to trade!"

"But, O stranger," said one, "if ye truly have come
seeking commerce, then where is thy stock?"
There was nowhere to hide on that plain bare and
wide,
not so much as a bush or a rock.

"Ah, thy question is cruel, for our calling is jewels
rich in hue, and so skillfully hewn
that the night, sick with shame at adornment so
plain,
threw away all the stars and the moons.

"Where we went, every crone ceased to slumber
alone
and the foulest-faced men would get wives.
We were set on," she sobbed. "All our riches were
robbed,
and we barely escaped with our lives."

On she went with the tale of imagined travail
and, expecting a bullet, I froze
thinking none could be swayed, that this feeble
charade
was like children at play in Pa's clothes.

But the customs of Mars hew but little to ours.
Hard and straight runs the road that they follow.
They will slay with a smile, but are strangers to
guile,
so the story she fed them, they swallowed.

James Hutchings lives in Melbourne, Australia. Two volumes of his 'Ideas and Inspiration For Fantasy and Science Fiction Writers' are now available from Amazon, Smashwords, Barnes & Noble and DriveThruFiction. James blogs regularly at http://www.apolitical.info/teleleli.

Evil rises deep in the Appalachian mountains, challenged only by a teenage witch... who doesn't believe in magic.

Adventure, fantasy, and folklore collide in Blood Creek Witch, an exciting new novel by Jay Barnson. Now available in eBook and paperback at major online booksellers.

Also available in Audiobook at Audible.com

Notes From the Nest

Well, this is it for Volume 1 of Cirsova. 10 issues certainly isn't bad! It's been a busy three years for us, and the future doesn't look any less busy as we move forward into 2019.

What does the future hold?

Volume 2, for one thing. Yes, we said it would be different, and in some regards it might be. I hope everyone isn't too disappointed, exclaiming "It's just more of the same!" when you open up our next issue and find the return of Schuyler Hernstrom, more of the adventures of Mongoose & Meerkat, and some other returning Cirsova favorites.

We're planning on putting out a new anthology of dark and horrific stories by Misha Burnett and Louise Sorensen, titled "Duel Visions". It's gonna be good! You'll want to check it out.

Of course, one of the projects we're most excited about is our Illustrated Stark series that will be released in time for the 70th Anniversary of Queen of the Martian Catacombs. Each of Leigh Brackett's novellas, originally published in Planet Stories, has been lovingly illustrated by StarTwo. You're going to want to get your hands on all of these!

I think that's going to keep our hands full for the next 12 months.

Importantly, I'd like to note that we will no longer be using Kickstarter to fund, nor will we be using IndieGoGo. We've never really *needed* crowdfunding platforms, though the boost from turning sales into events has probably helped us some. Unfortunately, Kickstarter's decision to block certain projects then leak communications with the creator to third parties has soured us on the platform. We had looked at IndieGoGo as an alternative, but in the wake of torpedoing Chuck Dixon's fully funded comic project for nebulous [and likely fabricated] TOS violations, we have opted not to use their platform.

Right now, we don't have many options, though we will be looking for them. Ultimately, however, we will not be using crowdfunding in the immediate future as a means of selling subscriptions. We hope that despite this you will continue to read and support Cirsova Magazine. We wouldn't be here without our readers, and for that, thank you!

P. Alexander, Ed.

www.ingramcontent.com/pod-product-compliance
Lightning Source LLC
Chambersburg PA
CBHW080752120626
46557CB00005B/1243